No part of this publication may be reproduced, stored in a retrieval system, or transmitted in any form or by any means, electronic, mechanical, photocopying, recording, scanning, or otherwise, without the prior written permission of the publisher, except in the case of brief quotations within critical reviews and otherwise as permitted by copyright law.

NOTE: This is a work of fiction. Names, characters, places, and incidents are a product of the author's imagination. Any resemblance to real life is purely coincidental. All characters in this story are 18 or older.

Copyright © 2018, Willow Winters Publishing. All rights reserved.

CARTER
&
ARIA

USA TODAY BESTSELLING AUTHOR

My grandmother used to write. Her dream was for her stories to be published one day, but unfortunately that never happened.

Times were different back then.

Although she's gone, she's always with me in my heart and even in my writing. Pieces of what I remember of my grandmother have been sewn into these stories and I hope that you've fallen in love with her, even if you've never had the pleasure to meet her. I hope she would be proud of me if she were to see me now.

The ones we love never leave us.
Mommom, this book is for you. I love you.

From USA Today bestselling author W Winters comes an emotionally captivating and thrilling, romantic suspense.

He holds a power over me like no one else ever could.

Maybe it's because my heart begs to beat in time with his. Maybe it's because my body bows to his and his alone. Maybe it's because he thought he loved me before he even laid eyes on me.

He thought wrong, it wasn't me he thought he loved, and nothing has made me suffer like that little secret has. He thought I belonged to him, but he was wrong. It was never supposed to be me.

Our memories are deceiving, but I know what I want now.
What I need more than anything.
I won't rest until he's as much mine as I am his.
It's always been him.

Endless

Prologue

Aria

I only know what Tyler looks like because of pictures. But even before then, when I first had the dream, I knew the boy was someone related to Carter. The Cross brothers all look so alike. He stared at me in the dream, his dark eyes piercing me even from across the field of blues and whites.

I should have been scared because I knew I didn't belong in this make-believe land conjured by my dream, but a soft smile lingered on his lips. Welcoming and endearing. He was kind. A kind soul among the flowers, although his words were anything but.

"She lied to you," he said casually. Words that etched confusion onto my face, but sent a prick of fear to chill my blood like ice.

It's only then that I heard my mother. I knew it was her instantly from her voice; we sounded so alike. A rustling noise came from somewhere on my right as she walked through the thick field. Her name begged to spill from my lips, rasping up from deep in my throat, but my voice was silent. And my body longed to move to her side, closer to where she was as she walked away slowly from me. But my limbs were still.

I was caught in place as they moved nearer one another, yet continued speaking to me, looking at me. As if they knew I was there even though I was held prisoner by whatever kept me immobile and quiet.

Tears leaked from the corners of my eyes and heated my skin as they rolled down my cheeks.

My father always spoke of my mother's beauty, and I knew it to be true, but she was older in the dreams than I remembered her to be. Age was more than kind to her though.

I tried to call out to her again, ignoring the boy, the Cross brother who had long since passed.

"I never lied," my mother spoke to me, but all I could feel was the way her words soothed my soul. It's been so long since I heard her voice. Too long. My fingers itched to move, to reach out to her and feel her embrace once more. I needed to be held so badly and my breath halted, imagining that she would come to me since I couldn't go to her, but she didn't.

Her hazel eyes were drenched in sorrow as she whispered, "I never lied to her." The biting wind carried her voice over the field.

As if her words were a cue, the sky darkened and dry lightning cracked it in two.

"Did you even love her?" the boy asked, looking up at her. "In all of this... did you even love her?" he asked my mother and the anger I felt was immediate, pushing the words up my throat although they still hung silent in the air. Of course she loved me. A mother always loves her children.

Even though the words had gone unvoiced, they both heard me and peered at me, judging my silent comment, but neither answered me. What I silently say to them changes each time the dream comes back, but the lack of an answer never does.

"Of course I did... I still do," she said and my mother's voice dragged with regret. "I died for her." She spoke clearly although pain riddled her words, and Tyler's expression only showed more agony as he shook his head.

With her head hung low, my mother pushed the hair from her face and delicately wiped the tears from under her eyes. The glossiness of her tears made her eyes more vivid and they called to me to ease her pain.

I've cried a thousand wretched screams, praying she could make out my words that I love her. That I miss her. But it doesn't change what happens next.

With the dark gray sky opening up and hard hail raining down on us mercilessly, pieces of the vision fall like a painting soaked in water. The colors smear and run together before fading to a blank canvas, and I'm left with nothing. Nothing but the sound of them arguing over her hate versus her love and what all really mattered the night she died. And another night... the night she changed the course of fate. She screams out that she died for me. Her confession is filled with a note of anger that burns through my veins.

But the last thing I always hear before I wake screaming, is her muttering, "We do stupid things for the ones we love."

No matter how many years pass, the nightmare never leaves me.

The first time it happened, I was in the cell. All those years ago when Carter, my love, first took me. But the visions have clung to me over the years, stained into my soul.

Chapter 1

Aria

"Don't scream."

With my breath caught in my throat, my body paralyzed from the rush of fear forced into every inch of my body, I hear the voice, but I don't obey.

My scream is muffled by his large hand and he holds me tighter, pulling me closer into his hard chest, his strong fingers digging into my skin.

The sound of his voice shushing me as I kick out, butting my head uselessly against the wall of muscle I'm pressed to— that sound is what calms me. I've heard it before.

Daniel.

My body relaxes slowly, barely held up by my weak legs. Adrenaline still courses through my veins, but consciously

I'm aware that it's him. The man who grabbed me and held me tight, *it's only Daniel*.

"Don't scream," he repeats, his lips close to the shell of my ear. So close that his warm breath tickles my neck and sends goosebumps down my shoulder. Too fucking close. He didn't just startle me; he scared the shit out of me.

I'm slow to remove my fingers from his forearm, one by one, knowing my sharp nails are digging into his arms. Blood is everywhere and so many stabs of pain race through my body, I'd rather be numb. Numb after everything that just happened.

It's only then that he loosens his grip and slowly moves in front of me, a hand still gripping my wrist.

"What are you doing?" The words rush from me in a single breath, but Daniel doesn't answer. As my heart pounds harder, he only observes me closely, noting my expression. The night air feels colder, and it's so much darker now that he's here than it was just a moment ago.

He looks behind me before meeting my gaze to ask, "Were you going to run?"

Of everything that he could have asked me just now, this question brings me more guilt than I'll ever admit. With Eli lying dead on the ground behind us, Addison upstairs somewhere, hiding from everything that's just happened, the fact I even thought about running makes me sick to my stomach. I could have. I could have run and left all of this behind like a horrid nightmare.

And I seriously considered it too.

"No," I whisper the word, not knowing if it's the truth or a lie. The nip of the evening air licks along my exposed skin as I stand in the open doorway of the safe house. The night is dark and unforgiving, much like Daniel's gaze. I can't hold it, knowing the emotions I'm feeling are written on my face.

Taking half a step back, I feel the pain of a small cut on my heel shoot up my leg, but it's nothing. Nothing compared to the pain of knowing what happened. All the small scrapes I got from the broken window, shattered from bullets, mean nothing.

War is here. The deafening sounds of gunshots have come and gone. But death has only just begun.

"What happened?" I voice the question with raw pain present in every whispered word. "Carter?" I ask him and open my eyes to meet his as they soften, then add, "My father?"

"Your father didn't come. Neither did Nikolai." His answer is clearly spoken and holds no pretense into what his thoughts are as his eyes roam over my face.

Before I can speak Carter's name again, feeling the familiar pain of loss already numbing my heart, he says, "Carter's fine. The Talvery men took a hit coming here. They should have known better."

Talvery men.

Men I'm supposed to be loyal to, and allies with. I don't know what to feel or who the real enemy is anymore. I just want it all to stop.

The breath I didn't know I was holding finally escapes, slipping through my parted lips as I lean against the doorway, letting the cool air drift along my heated face. But my throat is tight, the words and emotions tangled together and trying to escape me all at once.

"How many...?" I start to ask, but can't finish my question with the knot in my throat. *How many died tonight?*

"A lot," Daniel answers me and my eyes whip to his, demanding more. "Dozens, Aria."

I grip the top of my pajama shirt, balling the fabric together right at my chest, twisting it and wishing I could steal the pain away but it stays, growing with every beat.

I won't cry, even though a part of me wishes for nothing but to mourn. I've failed. And the very notion leads to a sarcastic response in the form of a hiss from the back of my mind. *As if you ever had the power to stop this.*

"Do you want to leave?" Daniel asks me, and the question is one I hold on to, craving the thought of running to take my mind elsewhere. Somewhere away from the thoughts of betrayal and mourning.

My lips part, but no words come out. Not at first. Daniel looks behind me once again, down the hall and to the front door of the large estate. He's waiting for someone to come, and I know deep in my gut this conversation needs to be finished before that person arrives. "I don't know," I answer him honestly and his gaze returns to me.

"You can go home. I'll make sure you get there safe. Or you can come back with us." He gives me the choice that's haunted me for weeks now. "There is no other way I leave you, Aria."

"Carter... he'll know you-"

"He thinks you're missing. He thinks your family took you back... or worse."

"They aren't my father's men." My head shakes vigorously, knowing he's speaking of the man upstairs and wanting to deny any ties to him. "That man was coming for us, both Addison and me, but I don't know him. I don't know who he is or what's going on, but he's not someone my father sent." Reaching out to him, I grab Daniel's jacket and he lets me, returning the gesture and shushing me once again.

"It doesn't matter. That's not the point." His words are more blunt and drenched with impatience I haven't seen from him before. Lowering my hand, I take a half step back as he tells me, "Right now, Carter thinks you've been taken by someone. But I can get you out of here, away from all this if it's what you want." My gaze falls to his throat as he swallows. The noises of the night are drowned out by the sound of my blood rushing in my ears at the thought of leaving Carter.

"You're offering me a way out?" *Thump*. My heart slams against my ribcage and I can't pinpoint which reason it's chosen in this moment to remind me it still exists. Either from the hope, or the fear of leaving.

Daniel only nods once before telling me, "Away from here and to your family, or wherever you want. You can go, Aria. I..." He struggles to complete his thought and turns away to cover his face with his hand before looking back at me. "I know you and Carter are on bad terms, and I..." He trails off again and swallows thickly before lowering his hand and looking me in the eyes.

He sees my pain, my agony; they're reflected in his dark gaze. "You can go. Or you can stay."

Chapter 2

Carter

Time moves too fucking slow. The drive back to Sebastian's place... every fucking roll of the tire is too goddamn slow.

If it weren't for the knowledge that I can pull the video feed from the security cameras on the property, evidence that will lead me to her, I wouldn't own a shred of sanity any longer. The phone in my hand is closer and closer to breaking as I bound up the steps and the anxiety grows. It's been in danger of breaking since the moment I first heard that Aria was missing. In danger of being splintered and thrown however far I could just to release the tension and pain still rippling inside of me at the thought of losing her.

"Where are the monitors?" I don't hide the anger in my tone the second the door is ripped open wide, Jase beside me, his footsteps barely keeping up with mine.

Before I can even scream at whoever's in here to get me the fucking tapes, I nearly trip over something on the floor. Stumbling forward, I barely catch myself. Eli. Fuck!

My throat closes and a sickness shoots through me. I can't help but reach to his throat and press my fingers against his icy skin. Even though he's cold, I still hope for a pulse. One second passes, and it hurts. Another second with nothing, and I can't fucking stand the cost of waging war. A war I choose to fight. All for her.

He's gone.

His eyes are closed and his blood is pooled around him. Jase has to step in a bit of blood to get around me and the bright red is smeared across the floor. We share a look as a few of our men come in behind us.

"Get him home." I give the command evenly, not revealing a shred of the emotions I'm feeling.

Control.

Eli dying is a reminder that I need control now more than anything. He will be missed and he will be mourned, but even he would tell me to focus on revenge right now.

"She's outside," Jase says and at first I don't understand what he's talking about until I turn to look over my shoulder. With the wind sweeping her locks off her shoulders and showing more of her skin, Aria glances at me.

She's here. She's safe. Relief is all-consuming for the

briefest of moments.

I have her.

Those beautiful hazel-green eyes of hers swirl with a mix of pain and regret. Not the relief I've been envisioning since I was told she was gone.

"She's here." The words leave me without consent, buried under my breath as I slowly stand.

"Carter." Daniel's voice carries across the hall as I make my way to them. He steps in front of her, but I still see her face, not daring to break her gaze as my pace picks up.

"Where were you?" I'm only half aware of how hard my voice comes out and that it echoes in the hall. My heart thuds painfully in my chest as I brush Daniel aside to get to her, gripping Aria by her shoulder to pull her inside and slam the door closed.

Her feet don't move fast enough, but I couldn't care less. *What the fuck is she thinking?* Having the door open is welcoming danger.

"What the fuck were you thinking?" I say, and the words come out with a vengeance. Hating that she'd put herself in danger and be so fucking stupid.

"Get off," she says as she pushes me away. In front of everyone, she looks back at me wild eyed and as if I'm the enemy. Like I'm the one who's to blame for every ounce of turmoil that wreaks havoc inside of me.

A numbness flows through me as I regard her, all while

she regards everyone else.

She wraps her arms around her shoulders and glances at my men behind me. It's then that I see what's captured her attention. The blood. It's everywhere. Soaked into the knees of their pants where they crouched on the floor and waited for more men to kill. Splattered on their shirts. My gaze falls to my own hands, stained with the blood of her family.

"I wasn't running..." Aria barely gets the words out before she stops and audibly swallows.

She doesn't run to me. She doesn't try to hold me. She glances at Eli and then pales.

As I look to my brother, the men behind me, and then to Addison slowly climbing down the stairs, the reality hits me.

She's still the enemy. She's not on my side. No matter how much I wish she were. *This war will break us.*

Aria's gaze travels the length of my suit, inventorying every bit of blood that's sprayed and spattered across it. Blood from men I've just killed.

I wish I knew what she was thinking. I wish I knew what to do.

Wrapping her arms tighter around herself, she looks at me with the silence surrounding us, suffocating us.

The only noise is the creaking of the stairs as Addison sneaks closer to Daniel.

"I wasn't running," she repeats. It sounds as if she regrets her words.

I don't know whether or not to believe her, but I know the feeling that seeps into my veins. Betrayal. And it comes from the woman I love, in the heart of war, in front of my brothers and army.

She left me once, and she'd do it again.

I imagined when I saw her, that she would run to me. That she would cling to me the same way I wish to cling to her.

The cold actuality is harsh and indisputable.

She's still a mistake – a drug I'm addicted to that's fucking up everything I've worked so hard for almost my entire life. I've never seen it more clearly than I do now.

If I didn't feel all of this for her, for a woman who chooses her family over mine, it would be all too easy. But why would she ever choose my family over hers? I don't know how I fell in love with her. It was nothing but a mistake.

It's in this moment I remember who I am.

A ruthless man with plans on tearing everything away from Aria's life, all because of who her father is and what destroying him does to her.

This isn't what I expected. I wanted to be her savior, her knight. But all I am is the fucking villain.

I'm as dead inside as I ever have been. And it's because of her. All of this bullshit is because of her. No, it's because I wanted her so badly I was willing to wage war, consequences be damned. Eli died, because of me.

"Whoever tried to take them knew her father was hitting

us tonight." I speak loud enough for everyone to hear and leave Aria standing where she is.

A slow tide of agony fills my gut and rises higher until I taste bile in my throat. "I want to see the security feed, now." Two men run off, heading for the stairwell that leads down to the basement.

"Is the house secure?" I ask Daniel and he hesitates to answer me, his eyes narrowing as he glances between Aria and me.

His gaze speaks a thousand words, most of them begging for me not to be the man I was forced to become, but I'm the one who had to bear that burden, not him. He has Addison.

I have no one. Not until Aria has no one left but me. And even then...

Finally, he nods. "It's secure to return but it'll take weeks to repair, or longer."

"All men back there," I tell him and then look Jase and the other men in the eyes. "Fix the mess her father caused."

Chapter 3

Aria

"You okay?" Jase asks me as we stand in the foyer of the Cross estate. Everyone was silent on the ride over here. Cars escorted ours in front and back, even on the sides when the road was wide enough. The security detail was hovering close around me, but it seemed more like guarding a prisoner than protecting an ally. Every minute that passed made me feel more and more like I didn't belong.

It made me feel like I'd made a mistake not leaving when I could have.

"Hey, you okay?" Jase asks me again as the men filter out of the foyer.

"You sure you should be talking to me?" I ask him in return and his huff of a laugh soothes a small part of my broken spirit. Without a doubt, I've fallen for Carter, but it wasn't until today that I realized how much I love his family too. Even while coated in the blood of my own family.

"It's tense, but everything will be all right."

"I don't know how you can think that," I answer him and my voice cracks. I know the men departing must hear how weak I am, and I hate it. This isn't the woman I want to be. Clearing my throat and focusing on the one thing I can confide in Jase about, I tell him, "He's angry with me."

"He was worried, Aria. We all were. We thought those men took you." It takes me a moment to realize what he's saying, to realize what Carter must've felt and guilt and insecurity weigh heavily against my chest.

So guilty. What have I done to bear all this guilt that has seeped into my gut?

"Besides, Carter's always angry." Jase tries to joke, to lighten the pain of what happened tonight. It doesn't help me though. There's nothing in this world that can help me now.

"I thought things were different," I whisper. But I didn't know this would happen. Deep down I knew it was coming, although I wanted to deny it. It's all coming to a head and I know I'm going to hate the outcome either way. There was never a thing that could have helped me. Not a damn thing that would have saved me. I'm a woman born to breed pain and misery. My last name demands it.

"We're still at war. A single battle was fought and men on

both sides died. It's going to cause tension."

"Tension," I scoff, although it's not meant to come out in an offensive way. It's just that tension isn't a strong enough word to describe the animosity and uncertainty stretching the space between us. The pure agony stifling both of us.

"Aren't you the one who called us the enemy?" Jase asks, reminding me of the words I told Eli only hours before his death. The memory sends a trickle of regret down my spine.

"Is that not what we are?" I ask him back in a low breath, peering into his eyes and wishing he would tell me otherwise. Even if it is a lie.

A beat passes, and there's nothing but silence. I wonder vaguely if the other men can hear. Or if Carter is maybe listening. If he even cares to listen at this point. He didn't speak a word to me in the car. He sat in the front, not in the back with me.

Jase only nods solemnly but squeezes my hand, then adds, "Falling in love with the enemy is torture." With a sad smile that doesn't reach his eyes, he lets go. I'm forced to watch him leave me, walking down the foyer, his footsteps echoing in the empty hall until my gaze lands on the photograph at the very end. The black-and-white shot of a house that feels as if it's lingered in the back of my mind. The importance of it, my thoughts long to remember.

If I had a choice, I'd go there now, just to see why the image haunts me. It has to do with Carter, I know it does.

And I need to know anything and everything that has to do with Carter.

Our families and pride may be at war, but not my heart. My heart belongs to him. I know it with everything in me. It's why I could never leave him, even if the option was handed to me so easily.

But in this moment, it feels as if he's ripped it from my chest and thrown it out in the cold, leaving it there to die. Covered in my family's blood and ripping me from the doorway, slamming it shut and screaming at me as if I'm a fool wasn't at all what I expected.

Whatever point he wanted to make in front of his men, I'm sure they heard it loud and clear.

He doesn't love me.

How many times have I said, "I love you," to him and I was given nothing in return?

A parched sensation blankets my throat, so dry it's futile to try to swallow.

The sound of heavy footsteps coming closer to me from the doorway at the end of the long hall, makes my body flinch with each step. They're brutal and dominating. They belong to Carter, no doubt.

Confirming my thought, the brooding beast enters the hall, a bottle of whiskey in his left hand and a tumbler with ice in his right. He doesn't bother to hide how pissed he still is. Pissed at me, judging from his acrimonious glare. Again I find myself unable to swallow, but I can't help confronting him.

"What did I do to deserve this?" I bite out the words as he starts to walk past me, down to the hall leading to his wing and presumably his bedroom or office. "What the fuck did I do but merely exist in the painful life I didn't choose?"

My heart batters against my chest while I wish to either run with fear, or beat him with pent-up rage. I'm not sure which.

Even though my own legs feel weak and numb from everything that's happened tonight, keeping me planted where I am, Carter's move forward as he ignores my question.

How fucking dare he ignore me.

With my ragged voice raised, I scream at him until my face is hot. "What did I do to deserve this?"

It only takes three strides before Carter's powerful presence is towering over me, and I nearly stumble backward. Nearly, but I keep my ground. I'm breathing chaotically and waiting for him to give me something. Anything is better than being ignored, made to feel like I don't even exist.

"Where do I start, *Miss Talvery*?" His voice is low as he moves down until his face is eye level with mine. He practically sneers my name and it shreds me from the inside. "You pointed a gun at me. You stand with your ex-lover and your father who have tried to kill me, not once, not twice, but every chance they get. Including the time one week ago, by said, fucking, ex, in which you knew what was happening but said nothing." The last word is sneered. He inhales deeply, pausing as pain rips through me.

I worry my bottom lip between my teeth before I bite down on it hard. The physical pain is vastly preferable to the emotional pain that boils inside of me at his aggressive attitude.

Carter already knew all of that when he fucked me the other night. When he held me like he loved me. Nothing has changed for me, and I don't deserve this. I love him. I've chosen him time and time again. The fact I'm still here after everything is proof of that.

"And then you tried to run," he adds and I whip my hand across his face. It's purely out of instinct, generated by his arrogance and the way I feel used and defiled by him. My palm smacks hard against his chiseled cheek and my fingers follow.

His face is like fucking stone. My hand throbs with a stinging, burning pain and as I wince, my eyes stay on Carter's unmoving expression. It didn't affect him in the least. All of the sickness and hurt that ache inside of me, I feel it all and he feels nothing.

Nothing.

"I didn't," I tell him, knowing I didn't try to run. It was only a passing thought and I won't be accused of anything more than that. Not when everything is stacked against us and I'm doing everything I can to stay by him. Even when he stands firmly against me.

Time passes and he merely stares at me, judging me, but I let him see the pain. I want to hide myself in this lonesome tower he's put me in, but I stand in front of him with my hands in fists by my side and beg him to feel what I feel. And to take it away.

"I don't deserve this, Carter," I say and my voice is strangled. *Please just take it all away.* I wish he could do that for me. However it entails, I don't want to feel this way for a second longer.

"I thought they'd taken you," he continues to talk with a look of disgust on his face, even though pain is etched into his words. "But you were just sneaking out to run away. What a fucking fool I was," he sneers.

"You are a fucking fool." I mimic his mocking tone, refusing to give him all of me when he chooses to believe otherwise. Holding my hand, which has started to go numb, I back away from him, knowing this battle is over and both of us have lost. "I wasn't running," I tell him the truth and then add, "And I won't say it again." The strength in my voice comes from some part of me deep inside. The part of me that knows I could stand beside this man. The part desperate to do exactly that.

His gaze assesses me, scrutinizing my expression.

"I'm not lying, Carter. I have no reason to lie to you." I let my voice soften, to show him the vulnerability. "I love you. Even through all this, I can't stop loving you. Yes, I had a chance to run, and I didn't take it. I wanted to stay with you."

My heart flickers in my chest, barely holding on to life as Carter's expression doesn't change, then another second passes and another.

"You don't believe me?" I say weakly with disbelief.

"You've hurt me once. Right there," he says then gestures with his hand behind me, to the hall that leads to the room where I held a gun to his head. "How can I believe you?"

"If you didn't think you could believe me," I say to try to numb the pain growing inside of me, like a ball of bile that drops in my stomach, "then why bring me back here?" All I can think is that he doesn't love me. He doesn't anymore.

Silence.

It's unbearably silent as my stomach churns while Carter walks off, leaving me without an answer. Without telling me that he loves me, even though I'm the fool who spoke those words to him.

Carter

My phone is constantly ringing, pinging, vibrating. Constantly distracting me from life itself and reminding me that I'm in control. It never lets up. Even now, the instant I turn notifications back on I'm flooded with alerts.

Every second the car moved and she said nothing—my Aria said nothing at all, not one fucking word to me or anyone else—every second of silence that passed only made the hate for what she'd done grow. She may not have been with her father or his men. But she sided with him nonetheless.

My phone goes off again, vibrating in my hand and it rattles against the cut crystal tumbler. With the adrenaline and anxiousness still ringing in my blood, my grip tightens, feeling the hard metal of the phone digging into my flesh as I open my bedroom door.

I need a fucking minute. One goddamn minute to take control again.

The incessant buzzing in my hand mocks me and I slam the door shut behind me, feeling my muscles tighten and the air thin as I struggle to keep my breathing steady.

Setting down the tumbler and bottle of whiskey on the dresser, I glance at my phone, unable to simply shut the fucking thing off.

It's Sebastian.

The intensity dims, the heat subsides. He always has a way of showing up when I need him most.

I heard what happened, his message reads and as I stare at his text, another comes in. *I know you'll probably say the same as always, that you don't need me to come back, but I have to ask. Do you want my help?*

I stare at the last line, taking in the word "want." When Sebastian left, it was a while before we talked again, given everything that changed the very next day. The day I had my unfortunate introduction to Aria's father.

I thought you were busy with Chloe and work? I write back then press send, still staring at the word "want."

He's asked a few times, when shit got rough over the years, if I needed him to come back.

"Need" being the operative word. And back then, knowing what happened between him and Romano, I never would have allowed him to come back and risk a damn thing. Not with a girl by his side. The girl who is now his wife, not to mention very much pregnant.

The guard job is over; it was just a summer gig.

He never stopped traveling. They moved from place to place when they ran from our hometown. He had enough money to keep them afloat until they found a bed and breakfast to hide away in, located on a huge cattle farm. He's been there for a while and it took him a long time, not until last year, nearly ten years after leaving this place to come back. The farm's shut down, the land's sold, and Chloe's pregnant. He has no reason to come back, not with the money he still has and the extra he makes doing security detail work. But I know he longs to come home, especially given Romano has no control here anymore. Even if he doesn't want to admit the one thing that's really held him back is Chloe.

I thought you said you and this city just don't mix. I can't help asking, pushing him away further and knowing full well what I'm doing.

Do I want him back? Yes. I need him now more than ever. Every piece of what I've built is crumbling and a part of me, the part that's very much alive, wishes desperately that

I could do what he did. That I could take Aria and simply run. To leave this shit behind, and make it just Aria and me. No one else, no problems, nothing but what we pack in a car before taking off. If I could trade places with him, I would.

But I have my brothers to look after, and consequences to suffer.

At one point, Sebastian was like the older brother I never had. And when he came here to see the safe house last year, I thought he'd stay. I should have known better. The world changed when he left, becoming darker, colder, and he didn't want it for Chloe.

I knew I was descending deeper and deeper into the pits of hell, a misery of my own making, when I watched them drive away. He said he'd be back, but it's been roughly a year. A year of messaging off and on. And a year that's changed everything.

I don't care what I said before. I want to come back, Carter. You need my help.

ARIA

It takes a long time for me to move from where Carter's left me. Daniel comes to check on me, to tell me Addison's in the study if I want company. He's not nearly as soft toward me as he was back at the safe house. I appreciate it either way though.

The thought of facing Addison though, knowing how she has Daniel and I don't have Carter... I can't take it right now.

Jase comes by again, although he doesn't speak. He only squeezes my shoulders and offers me a weak smile that I return with a shake of my head.

Even Declan comes by and tells me he'll make me something to eat if I want, but I know I would throw it up if I could even manage to take a bite of anything at all.

It takes me a long, long time before I start walking down to Carter's wing. The idea of staying in the hideaway room offers a small bit of comfort. I could be alone and break down where the only person who would see is Carter, if he bothered to check on me.

But I don't want to hide – even if I do want to be alone. Time is precious and I don't want to live like this.

I'm halfway to Carter's bedroom when my pace picks up. His door is closed, and I'm scared it will be locked when I grip the carved glass knob, but it turns easily for me.

Too easily, even.

The savage man I love is standing at his dresser, the whiskey bottle still sealed in front of him. But shattered glass scatters moonlight around the room as the curtains sway from the air blowing through the vents, letting in glimpses of the light.

It looks as if he must've slammed the glass down too hard and with another step into the room, my eyes assessing his hand as I close the door behind me, I can see the cuts that line his skin.

From the glass, or from earlier today, I'm not sure. Maybe the mixture of wounds is from both. The reminder he's killed men today, men who may have protected me in the past, men who I've had dinner with, men who have fought for my father for years, settles an eerie chill in my bones as the door clicks shut and Carter's dark eyes peer back at me from over his shoulder.

There's a slam of fear in my chest, but it's gone quickly as Carter turns his head forward again toward the bottle, not even bothering to look at me for more than that split second.

And then I'm given more silence.

In that moment, I almost turn and walk away. I almost run out of the room. Almost... but I don't. I have a voice, and I'm going to use it.

"I'm not going to stay here as a prisoner. If you don't want me, I'm leaving." I don't know how I manage to say the words so clearly, but I do. I hold on to that small accomplishment as Carter answers me.

"I have a right to be angry." There's no menace in his voice at all. Merely truth.

"You don't have a right to treat me like I'm nothing," I dare to respond with a harshly spoken whisper.

"Did it even cross your mind that maybe I was dead?" he asks, slowly turning to face me. His eyes are tired and his voice wretched.

"Yes," I answer him quickly as my breathing catches in my chest, remembering all the worry the gunshots crying out in the night brought me.

"And what did that do to you?"

"It made me angry... angry that you didn't call." I swallow thickly, remembering how I held the phone. "I messaged you and you didn't bother to give me any sign at all that you were all right or that you cared." I confess a raw truth, baring more of myself to him, "And it hurt in every way possible. Every piece of me went numb thinking you were out there... that you were gone like Eli was." It feels wrong even speaking of Eli right now. His memory should be honored and not brought up like this.

"Daniel had already told me you were all right." I hope that truth eases something in him as I realize at least one of the reasons why I'm angry. "I knew you were all right and even if I was mad that you were ignoring me, I promise you I couldn't have felt more relief at finding out that you were okay." Every time I turn soft for him, I lose that hard edge that makes me his equal. I know it, yet I do it every time.

Carter's quiet for what seems like an eternity, as if registering what I may have been feeling for the first time. Please, I pray he'll understand. With so much against us, we need to understand each other if nothing else.

"I thought you were dead and I was ready to kill anyone

who stood in my path to find you, Aria. And yet, when I got there, you didn't..."

"I didn't what?" I question him with a raised voice, begging him to tell me everything. With a hesitant step forward, I stop when he answers.

"You didn't react to seeing me."

"What did you want from me?" I ask him, honestly not knowing what he wanted. "You grabbed me like I was a child acting up." Instinctively, my hand moves to my forearm where he ripped me from the doorway and yanked me inside of the house.

"You didn't even ask if I was all right," he spits at me, condemning me for not comforting him when I'd just witnessed more death firsthand than I ever have in my life.

"There was death everywhere around me, and I knew my family was out there but-"

"It's your family you care about!"

I'm taken aback by the venom in his words. "You already knew I loved them and that I didn't want this-"

"I would do anything for you. I would kill for you. I feel like I would die without you. Yet when I got to you... all you wanted was for me to let you go."

"Carter, you don't understand."

"No, I don't." His answer is hard and unmoving.

"I'm sorry," I say, giving him an apology I truly mean. "I didn't want to upset you; I'm just not okay right now... and I was even worse earlier."

Carter's expression softens slightly, but I can tell he's holding on to his reservations. I know he doesn't trust me. I've lost his trust completely and it makes me feel trapped and desperate, needing him to give me a chance.

"I'm sorry. Do you believe me?" My question is pleading as I take the few small steps needed to stand in front of him. I swear he can hear my heart pounding as I dare to tell him, "If I could go back, I would. I would make sure I gave you what you needed, even as I dealt with all of this... this agony inside of me."

I'm careful as I raise a hand and cup his jaw. His five o'clock shadow is rough against my fingertips. The anger wanes from him as I rub my thumb up and down his cheek.

"I'm sorry. I didn't want any of this to happen, but I don't want to lose you." My words slip from me easily, raw, transparent and true. I mean every word of it.

Carter takes a step to his left, closer to the bed and says under his breath, "There's no room to be sorry in this life."

Crying is something I'm done with. I swallow down the spiked pain and embrace it rather than succumb to weakness. A second passes as Carter strips out of his shirt, unbuttoning it and then tossing it onto the floor.

He may have grabbed me earlier as if I was a defiant child walking out recklessly into a busy street, but right now, he's the one acting like a child.

"You just want to be angry with me, don't you?" I pause my thoughts as he removes his cotton undershirt, stained with blood too. "There's nothing I could say or do to change your mind. You want to be pissed at me."

He looks at me from over his shoulder, a derisive glance. "Why would I want that, little songbird?"

"Because if you aren't angry, you'll have to deal with everything else that's brewing inside of you. If you aren't a beast, then you have to be a mere mortal and deal with what you're feeling." I spew the words, not even conscious of them until they've left me.

"Ever the artist, aren't you?" He makes light of the truth, not willing to admit how accurate my words are as he turns to me and stalks closer, wearing nothing but his pants. His hardened muscles ripple in the dim light and his dark eyes seem bright with a challenge.

"Make light of it all you want. You simply want to be angry with me." He takes a large step forward and I take a small one back, not letting him get close enough to touch me. "And I'm fine with it, so long as you know it's bullshit and that I'm very aware of what bullshit it is." I spit out the last words, hating him for what he's doing. He's using his rage as a buffer to maintain his veneer of control. And it's not fair. "I love you, Carter Cross. I chose you." I have to add in the last statements, if for no other reason than to be honest with myself. Even now, I still love him. He's ruthless; an uncaring and brutal asshole. And I'm the fool who loves him and wants him to give up a piece of his armor, knowing I'll protect that part of him with everything I have.

"You didn't choose me," he insists and I start to respond, but he continues. "Choose me now, and kneel."

My pulse quickens at the look in his eyes. I've seen it before, so many times. And I'm grateful for the change. Hopeful to reach the man I love through this veil of hate.

I look him in the eyes as I obey him. The blood that rushes through my veins heats with desire. There wasn't a single part of me that hesitated.

He crouches in front of me, bringing him to eye level, and my gaze stays pinned to his. The depths of his dark irises ignite with power, with a primal need.

Take from me, Carter. Take what you need and what's left of me will still love you.

Spearing his fingers through my hair, he makes a fist and forces my head to tilt. My breath hitches with the sudden grip, and my body bows to his. There's barely a hint of pain; it's merely him taking control as he crashes his lips to mine. My hands reach up instinctively, bracing either side of his jaw as he ravages me.

The kiss is everything. It's warmth. It's home. It's a touch that awakens the pieces of me that have been silent and waiting for him to come back. I moan into his kiss, wishing I wasn't in this position so I could lean into his hold, so I could take more of him and show him how desperate I am for us to go back to what we were.

But there's no way we could ever go back.

You can never go back.

My lips feel swollen and bruised by the time he releases me, slowly loosening his grip. My chest heaves for air, and I love it. When I peek up at him, my vision hazy with lust, I see his eyes closed and his own lips parted as he takes in a steadying breath, then opens his eyes to pin me in place.

The gaze of a hunter, a predator even, stills my beating heart.

In the pale light of the early morning trickling through his curtains, the soft shadows line his jaw and make him look even more domineering.

He stands slowly, leaving me where I am and I can see his thick length as he does, pressing against his pants.

He paces in front of me, deliberating on what to do next, and I'm eager to find out.

"You'll pay for what you did."

"What I did?" The question is spoken with confusion. I have to blink away the desire as fear creeps in.

"Raising a gun to me. Standing in opposition to me." He doesn't hold any anger in his words. Only truth and certainty.

"I thought I already did." My voice is choked as I gasp out the words.

"You lost my trust."

I can only nod, not trusting myself to speak. I think about

everything he's done to me since the first night I laid eyes on him. How he's deprived me, lied to me, locked me away and punished me with both pleasure and pain.

"Holding grudges hardens the heart," I murmur to myself, but my words are for him as well.

"I don't have a heart, songbird." His response is quick, but so is mine.

"I don't like it when you lie to me."

It's quiet for a moment. Carter's mind is made up for tonight. But we have time. I don't know how much, but there's always hope. And I know my soul speaks to his. My soul is desperate to stay with his. It's the only truth that matters. *I need him*.

"If you're staying in my bed tonight, you're going to have to satisfy me." As Carter speaks, my gaze is drawn to his strong jaw and then to his throat. I watch as his chest rises and falls and he stands in front of me, unbuckling his belt. The sound of the leather hissing in the air as it's pulled through the loops makes my pussy heat and clench.

"I'm staying with you," I tell him with a mix of defiance and the greedy need to be taken by him. I can't help but think he just needs to be touched. To be loved. To be given free rein over me and to *feel* how much I need him. *This* is what we need.

He doesn't speak as he unzips his pants and then lets them fall to the floor with a soft thud.

His cock bobs in front of me, swollen and each vein protruding. I can practically feel his thickness pulsing inside of me already. He may need this, but I know I need it too. I need to be loved. Loved for the person I am, by this man and this man alone.

"Lie on the bed on your belly," he commands me and I'm eager to move.

I want to make this right between us however I can.

And if this is how he chooses, to command me, defile me, degrade me in his bed, I'll obey him without objection. Because I fucking love it too.

As I crawl up the bed, stripping as I go and tossing the clothes on the floor, I hear Carter open a bedside drawer. I'm not sure what it is he's getting, but I don't care. I just want him. However I can get him.

With a cheek pressed to the pillow, I lie still on the bed, naked and waiting for him to do as he pleases. I know he won't hurt me. Not like this. His words are venomous, and his deprivation of affection is torturous, but here, like this, he won't hurt me. I know he won't. Whether he says it or not, a piece of him loves me more than his entirety could ever hate me.

The bed dips in time with my heart at the thought, and Carter climbs on top of me, his hard erection digging into my thigh as he leans over me. His fingers trail up my side and make my whole body shiver. He gently pulls back the hair over my ear to kiss my neck, giving me goosebumps that cause my nipples to harden and a shudder to run down my shoulders.

"You think you love me, Aria," he whispers in a threatening tone that turns my blood to ice. "Let me show you exactly what kind of a beast I can be."

Letting my hair fall back into place, he sits up straighter and the air around me suddenly feels colder without him there any longer.

My heartbeat quickens, but I ignore the lingering threat and welcome whatever he wants to do to me. He is mine, and I am his.

A click sounds in the air at the same time a sudden coldness hits my ass. It's wet and slick, and it takes me a moment to realize what it is.

Carter drizzles lube over my ass and then runs his finger down to my forbidden entrance. Heat rolls through my body and I struggle to stay still, knowing what he's going to do.

He takes his time, teasing me, stretching me, pushing himself in and out for what feels like too long. I can't take it. I can't stand waiting any longer, knowing what he wants and what he's going to take from me.

"Carter," I say and his name is a plea on my lips. My head moves from side to side as he shushes me.

He presses his head inside of me and it's already too much. I jump away from him, my teeth clenching.

"Push back," he commands me and then adds as he slips inside of me, "Push back right now."

My hips tilt up slightly, although only because of his grip on them and I do what he says, but it's so much. Too much. My body blazes with the forbidden touch.

I'm so hot. So full already. Every inch of my skin tingles as I try not to writhe underneath him. With one of his hands on my hip and the other gripping my shoulder with a bruising force, he slams all of himself inside of me in a swift, unforgiving thrust.

The pain of being stretched this way for the first time forces me to bite down on the pillow as tears flood and sting my eyes. I can feel him pulse inside of me, growing harder and larger and it's too much. It's all too much.

My body's on fire, alternated with freezing cold as he moves behind me at a slow, but relentless pace.

"Carter," I whimper his name as the overwhelming sensation begs me to move away but then, with just as much need, to push back and take more of him this way.

My clit rubs against the comforter beneath me and I moan. A single moan of utter pleasure, my body choosing it over the pain. Carter takes it as his cue to pick up his pace, ruthlessly fucking my ass and shoving my body down into the bed with each hard pump.

"Fuck," I moan out and he responds with a low groan from deep in his chest.

My fingers dig into the comforter, my nails scratching along the threads as my head thrashes and I struggle to breathe.

Pleasure and pain mix in a cocktail I'm already drunk on.

He whispers at the shell of my ear, "You're such a dirty whore for me." At the same time, he shoves his fingers inside of my pussy and presses his thumb to my clit.

Holy fuck!

My mouth hangs open with a silent scream of ecstasy. The pleasure ripples through my body and paralyzes me as he thrusts behind me, pistoning his hips and filling me to the point where it's nearly too much with both his fingers and his cock. I've never felt like this. So full, so hot, so consumed by bliss.

He fucks me harder once my orgasm begins to wane. He doesn't stop, not even when he sinks inside of me so deep that I feel like he'll split me in two. I try to spin around out of instinct and push him away.

Instantly, Carter stops. Barely keeping himself inside of me, he tells me with a cold gaze, "Keep your hands down." There's no desire in his voice, no sense of mercy or love. Nothing but anger that I've dared to push him away.

It's a shock to my system. Seeing him like that while I feel nothing but desire and love is sobering. An icy gust sweeps through me even as he changes his expression, softening it and gently pushing my shoulders back to the bed.

"It's too much," I whisper and although the pain is gone, the intensity of what we had has vanished.

"Lie back down," he commands me in a way that leaves a

deep fracture in my heart. I can hear it splinter as I return my cheek to the pillow.

He doesn't touch me again; he doesn't resume fucking me. He doesn't allow himself to cum.

Instead, he gets up and moves away from me. I try to keep from crying as the pleasure from my orgasm withers to nothing while he enters the bathroom and flicks on the light.

I feel alone in this moment, broken and used. Utterly alone. It reminds me of the last time we were together, of him tying me up and not fucking me. Instead he left me after torturing the truth out of me.

Is that all this was? More torture?

I stay still as he wipes me down and returns to the bathroom. My chest feels hollow and it's hard to swallow. Maybe I didn't lose him tonight. Maybe I lost him that night when I told him I would never forgive him. Maybe I lost him the moment I picked up the gun and I've only just now seen it.

All I know right now is that I feel like I've lost him.

Refusing to cry, I bite the inside of my cheek and listen to him walk back to the bed after turning off the light. The bed creaks as he gets in beside me. He doesn't crawl under the sheets he laid on top of me, and I don't move from where I am. I'll wait for him.

He loves me. I know he loves me, but why does it feel like he doesn't at all? *Why do I feel like I'm lying to myself?*

"I love you," I whisper and chance a look at him. The sun

has risen and he can't hide in the darkness. His eyes are tired and his face looks older than it ever has before.

I watch his throat bob as he lies back in the bed and says nothing. He says nothing.

More silence. And that's the last bit I can take.

Licking my dry lips, I realize his intention was simply to hurt me, at least in that moment I turned around, the moment where it was too much. I'm quick to get up and move away from him, pushing the sheets aside.

His grip is hot, burning into me as he wraps a strong hand around my hip and pulls me into his hard, chiseled chest.

"You know I care for you." He says the words sternly, but he doesn't look at me. Not at first. The pounding in my chest rises to my throat until his eyes find mine, swirling with pain.

The chaos warps and twists inside of me. I'm hurting for him, a man who feels betrayed and doesn't know what to do because every time life has given him a challenger, he's simply murdered them, yet here I stand.

But I'm also in pain. For falling for a man so merciless and heartless as Carter.

"Don't ever do that again," I say, barely keeping my voice from breaking. "Don't ever treat me like I'm nothing to you."

"Is that a threat?" he asks, still not looking at me.

"No. Not a threat, a promise. Carter, look at me." My voice sharpens and his eyes find mine. "If you ever do that again, I'll leave you." It takes everything in me to tell him that, because I know it's true. And I'm worried it will happen. It feels so close to being inevitable.

"Do what exactly?" he asks me, daring to play as if he doesn't know. As if he doesn't realize how much he's hurt me tonight.

"Fuck me just to prove how willing I am for you to have me. Walk by me as if I'm meaningless in your life." I nearly choke on my last words, remembering how I felt in the foyer. "Treat me like I'm not worth sparing a glance."

"First, I wanted you. I fucked you because I wanted you." His tone is sharp until he adds, "But something... changed."

"Something?" I ask him, but he doesn't answer me. He keeps on speaking as if I hadn't voiced the question at all.

"What was it like to hold a gun to my head?" he asks, and his voice is thick with emotion. "Did you think it made me feel like I meant something to you?" He doesn't hide the pain behind a mask of cold indifference. I can hear him swallow and for the first time, he shows me everything in his expression. I've hurt him so deeply and I didn't even know.

"Carter, don't..." I start to say, inching closer to him although he stays perfectly still. "I was just trying to survive," I say, begging him to understand. "If I could take it back-"

"You wouldn't," he cuts me off, and I know he's right. Under that circumstance, I wouldn't allow him to murder my friends and family. It's fucked up how much that very knowledge guts me. There's no way for me to make it out of this alive.

"You were just surviving. Maybe pretending that you mean nothing to me is a way for me to just survive."

I'm struck by his confession, and I hate it. I hate the lives we have, and how fate has put us in each other's path.

"Please don't do this, Carter." My throat is tight as despair claws its way up. "I know we're broken, but stop this. Don't do this again. Don't make it worse."

"I can't make it better," he rebuts.

"Tell me you care for me again," I whisper, getting closer to him and ignoring the pain that still lingers. When I walked back into Carter's grasp, easily letting him take me back here, I had no idea that we were so broken. How could I have been so fucking foolish to think that loving him was going to fix it all? As if it could put a stop to the war, rewrite the past, and make us invincible for whatever lies ahead.

He tells me he cares about me after a moment, but then he tells me a truth I hadn't dared to admit I already knew until he spoke the words. "I wish I didn't. It would all be easier if I didn't."

Chapter 4

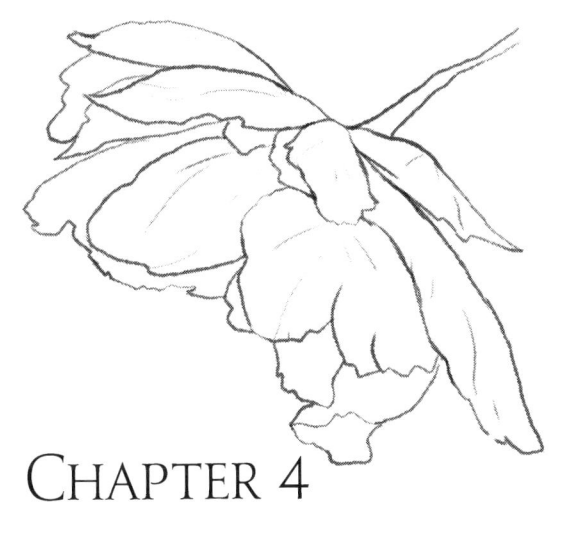

Carter

Every time I thrust inside of her, I remembered the confessions she made the other night. How she told me she'd be with Nikolai if I wasn't in the picture, and how she'll never forgive me. She meant them. She still does.

Being inside of her is heaven, but last night, it was hell. There was no way I could have taken any pleasure in her. Not when all I can think is how she's going to hate me when this is over. There's no way I'm going to be able to keep her. It's fucking impossible.

A numbness spreads through my hand as I form a fist, letting the cuts split open and feeling the pain rip through my knuckles. Leaning back in my office chair, I clench and unclench my hand again and again, just to feel something else.

I've never wanted to forget so much. To erase the mess I've gotten us into. To run away with her and start over.

It's a pain I've never felt and a position I never considered I'd be in. Because I've never felt this way about anyone else. No one else has meant so much to me before. Not even my brothers.

I don't know how we're going to make it out of this together. And I've never wanted anything more.

The long strand of pearls that starts out with small spheres growing in size until they reach the center, stares back at me from its velvet box on the desk. The iridescence shines off the polished pearls, stealing my gaze. They mesmerized me, as did my Aria. Anything that can keep my attention should belong to her.

I needed to replace her previous necklace with one she could wear forever. This necklace is timeless and even if she leaves me, I pray she'll keep it forever. I pray that what we had will be endless, even if us being together is only a dream I could dare to return to in my sleep.

As I hear Aria's footsteps patter closer to my office right before the door creaks open, I shut the velvet box. Aria's eyes are still puffy and red from lack of sleep, and her lips are swollen. She grips her sleepshirt with one hand and playfully knocks on the door even though it's open and our eyes have already met.

She attempts a smile, but it disappears as quickly as it came.

Fuck, it hurts. I want nothing more than for her to be happy. Truly happy with me, with the man I am and will always be.

"I wasn't sure if you wanted me to dress," she barely speaks before adding, "since there weren't any clothes laid out."

I watch her throat as she swallows, and again she balls the thin cotton of her sleepshirt in her hand. She doesn't wear it in bed, only when she leaves the bedroom. The tension in the air is thick, and it makes my fingers go numb again and prick with anguish.

"You still want me to?" I ask her and she nods swiftly and without hesitation. I love this submissive side of her, this trusting side. I love that she wants this side of me. Even more, I love that I can so easily give her what she wants.

"I like it when you do things like that," she answers.

With a single nod, I stand up and make my way to the other side of the desk, swallowing down the lump and remembering that I need to be in control at all times. For her, and for the sake of my family and everyone else relying on me. Aria stands where she is, looking lost and insecure.

I hate it, even though I know I'm the reason for it all. I could easily bring her back into my arms and love her. But it would only end in her hating me, in her breaking me and destroying the last bit of my sanity.

If it ends this way, slowly, and with a growing chasm between us, it'll be easier to accept. For both of us.

"For you," I say and hold out the black box for her to take, and only then does she step forward. As the box creaks open, I move the chair to face her and take a seat, explaining as my back hits the smooth leather, "It's your birthday gift."

She forces a small smile to her lips, but the sadness lingers there. "It's beautiful," she says, although she doesn't look at me. "What happened to my other... necklace?" Instinctively, her hand reaches for her collar, to the place where the diamonds and pearls used to lay.

"It's where you left it," I tell her and then glance at the box, still pushed against the wall but not lined up exactly with where it normally goes. I don't want it to go back to where it was. I want to remember. I *have* to remember. My gut churns at the memory of how I felt, sitting in this very chair, while she locked herself in that box. I'm sickened by all the hate and anger I had, but more than that, the realization that what I wanted would never be.

"Are we okay?" Aria's gentle question, laced with both want and fear, brings my attention to her gorgeous face.

"I don't know that we'll ever be okay." My answer is instant and calmly spoken as if it's a certainty. "But that doesn't make you any less mine."

"I don't know what I can do, Carter." Aria's voice is wretched as she stares at the pearls, her fingertips barely skimming along each one. "I want to make this right."

"This was never going to be right, Aria. It wasn't right what I did, and what I'm going to do... it's not right to you." I don't like the way my words come out. As if I'm letting her go, because I'm not. I won't be the one to break things off, but I know she'll leave me.

It's inevitable.

"You don't get to decide what's right for me." Her answer is sharp, that defiance I love slicing through the painful truth even she can't deny: We were never meant to be.

"You're still angry at me, aren't you? For grabbing the gun." Her voice wavers as she adds, "I'm sorry, Carter." Her words are rushed and she barely breathes as she takes a single step toward me, closing the space until I reach out to take her waist in my hands. I could pull her into my lap, but I don't. I keep her right where she is, at arm's length.

"I know you are," I tell her solemnly.

"Does this mean you don't forgive me?" The pain isn't hidden in the least. Not in her words, or the way her hands hold on to mine, not in the shades of amber and jade in her eyes.

"It's not about forgiveness, Aria. I understand why. I respect it, even. But it would happen again. You would do it again." I speak to her without reservations. She'll come to the same realization I have. She will, even if it hurts her with the same pain it does me.

"You're the one who put me here. Who put me right in the middle, Carter. You could lock me in the cell, and then I wouldn't be in the way." She pleads with me, wanting me to take away her freedom and the woman she was always meant to be just so I can have her.

"You're the one who wanted out of your cage to fly away. Isn't that right?" I know it doesn't change anything. Giving her freedom only to be disappointed with what she does with it, doesn't change a damn thing between us.

"You're the one who didn't clip my wings," she says and the hazel concoction in her eyes begs me to fall for her. To give in and simply love her. They don't know it, just as she doesn't. I already do. I love her with everything in me. But this is all I can offer her. I'm already giving her everything I have. "You let me find you. You gave me that choice... I know you must've," she tells me and I don't deny it.

"To clip your wings... to keep you out of it all... that would have been the greatest of crimes, my songbird."

Chapter 5

Aria

I haven't left the hideaway room in ... I don't know how long.

The pearls are still on my pillow, where I left them. Both the strand of pearls Carter gave me this morning, and the loose pearls and diamonds I retrieved from the box in his office. He left me standing there, knowing we were broken beyond repair. And I did my best to clean it up. Picking up the evidence of my broken collar all while hot tears slid down my cheeks and fell into the box where I lay only a week ago.

I know the pain of a love being over. It's an undeniable feeling that stretches out slowly through each limb and finger. It's numbing, yet unforgivingly sharp.

My chest heaved with each sob until I fell to the floor.

Love isn't enough, and that's the worst thing in the whole

world. Love is supposed to conquer all. It's supposed to persevere. Instead all it's done is caused us both unbearable pain. A pain I would do anything not to feel ever again.

I've lain in the makeshift bed, a pile of pillows on top of the plush rug, warring with myself. I've thought every possible situation through. Ranging from walking into the cell willingly and locking it behind me until it's all over, to telling Carter I'd kill my father and Nikolai with my own two hands.

And I hate the woman in each scenario. I despise her. And I also know I would never be able to live with myself. I would simply be waiting until the day I died. Living each moment with a resentment toward Carter that I don't think I could hide.

Fate is cruel, and this world is colder than I ever imagined.

My body is sore and it takes a moment when I stand up to begin to move. I haven't had anything to drink or eat in … I don't know how long. I'm dizzy and there's a pounding in my temple that won't quit.

I move slowly to the kitchen, listening to my bare feet pad softly on the floor and breathing in and out as deeply as I can. A cup of coffee is what I'm after, a piping hot cup that's mostly sugar and cream. I only need the coffee for the caffeine. But what I get are the sounds of Addison and Daniel carrying from the kitchen to the hallway.

I stop just outside the doorway, listening to Addison tell Daniel how she'll never leave him again.

"You promise?" Daniel's voice is soothing and there's a smile that's hidden in his voice; I can see in my mind the exact smile that would play at his lips.

"I don't want to run away anymore." Addison's voice is nothing but sincere. "Nothing will come between us, Daniel. If we can make it through that…"

My cheek rests on the outside of the doorway as I listen to them, feeling the love between them that's always been there.

I can't help but feel a pang of jealousy and to wish it were that easy for Carter and me.

"Then marry me." Daniel's response makes my eyes widen and suddenly I feel like an intruder. Not at all like a friend or family. I'm only an eavesdropper who needs to go away and not stain their memory, even if they don't realize it.

Her voice is soft as she tells him yes between quick kisses I can hear even as I push away from the doorway. Turning around, I feel nothing and everything all at once. Jealousy and happiness. Emptiness from knowing I'll never have what they share, and a sense of completion for accepting it.

Is this what it feels like to completely break down?

With a single deep breath, my eyes closed and my muscles tight, I take a step forward only to be hit by the heat of a hard body as I walk forward.

My pulse quickens when I open my eyes.

"Lost?" Carter's voice isn't muted like my footsteps were, and I can hear Addison and Daniel come out from the kitchen and into the doorway to the hall.

My body's stiff, and it takes a moment for me to even gather the courage to look over my shoulder at them.

I don't belong here. It's never been more apparent to me. I shouldn't be here.

"Aria," Addison's quick to call out for me, but I can't even stand to look at her knowing we couldn't be any further apart in what we're feeling right now. She doesn't need me dragging her down, ruining this special moment for her, and there's nothing she can give me in this moment that I would accept.

"I'm good," I say and barely turn to look over my shoulder at the only friend I have in here. With my hand raised, she stops where she is. "Please." The single word is a plea for her to leave me alone, and she listens.

Stepping around Carter, I leave them as quick as I can. I only glance back once to see Daniel holding Addison's wrist as she stares at me with tears in her eyes. Carter's gone; where to? I don't know, and I don't care.

I've never felt so torn in my life.

I knew life would never be easy for me. Not with the man my father is. But I never imagined I'd fall in love with the enemy. So much so that I would be here with him, willingly, while my family mourns deaths committed by his hand. Or that I would be mourning the loss of a love that never should have been.

So what does that make me?

Who does that make me?

Chapter 6

Carter

War stops for no one.

Death never waits.

"Each wing is secure and the repairs are underway, sir," Aden tells me with a nod of his head as he stands outside of Jase's office in his wing. Most of the damage was done to Declan's wing, but everything is salvageable.

"What's the timeline?" I ask Aden. He's a new guard, one of a dozen. When the death toll came in, we lost more men than I thought originally. Right now we're keeping everyone close, but it's only temporary; it's just until we get eyes on both Romano's men and Talvery's. Jett's taking care of that with a small crew. Everything's waiting on him. But I fucking hate waiting.

"Two weeks tops until everything is replaced," he answers and I give him a nod, effectively dismissing him before walking into Jase's open door and closing it behind me.

Jase's office is nothing like mine. There's not a single book. There's no desk either. I only refer to it as an office because he does. The fireplace is almost always lit though, and flames reflect off of the mirrored coffee table in front of it. The mirrored surface has a thick patina that's developed over time. I guess Jase prefers it that way, or he'd polish it.

The shelves that line the wall to the right hold the rare antique weapons he collects. Mostly swords and knives. The ancient feel they have and their crude primitive backgrounds are at odds with the clean lines of the rest of the room. Overall, the aesthetic is modern and barren.

"How is she?" Jase asks me. His gaze stays on the fire until I take the seat next to him on the sleek, black leather sofa. It's only then that he looks up at me.

I don't answer him, the words fighting with my emotions in the back of my throat.

"That bad?" he asks, and I only nod.

The fire crackles in front of us while I sit with my brother, remembering how we got here nearly a decade ago. When I was only a kid, left at death's doorstep and wishing for it to come quickly. Jase is the one who made the first move. He killed each of the men who grabbed me from the street corner. He was fueled by anger alone, but when I recovered and learned what he'd done, I knew there would be far more death before that anger would be allowed to leave him.

One by one, we killed, we stole, we ruled with a fear we once had for others.

But fear has a way of changing you. And I would be a liar to say I wasn't motivated by it now.

I'm afraid I'm going to lose the only woman worth fighting for. The only woman I'm capable of loving.

The thick leather groans as Jase leans back, rubbing his thumb over his jaw and tells me, "It'll be all right when this is over. She'll be all right in time."

"Or she'll be consumed by anger," I say and give him a knowing look, but the expression on his face doesn't waver.

"She loves you," is his only response.

I break his gaze to stare at the fire, wondering how long it'll take for a flame so high and hot to burn down to nothing but ash and smolder.

"I didn't come to talk about her."

"It's all about her, isn't it?" he questions and my chest tightens. If I could go back to that moment and tell him not to fight for revenge, if I could go back and instead take my brothers and leave that horrid place, I would. I'm not proud of who we've become and I know it's because of me.

"You know what I mean," I tell him rather than lying to him and pretending I didn't get us into this shit because of a sick need to have Aria to myself.

"What did you come to talk about then?" Jase asks and then lays his head back. He picks up a knife from the table and plays with the blade between his fingers.

"What do you want to do from here?" I ask him. The fight in me is subdued and he can see it. I'm certain everyone can. I've never felt so weak in my life.

"I say we wait," he offers, staring into the roaring fire. The flames dance in the darkness of his eyes.

"We could hit them now... Let the streets run with blood," I suggest to him, knowing the day is coming soon. That's how this works. The winner takes the final blow.

"Two reasons. The first is that Sebastian is coming back."

Sebastian. My initial reaction to hearing that he's coming back is nothing I expected. I feel as if I've failed him. I'm ashamed for him to come back and see me like this. Ever since Aria came here, I've messaged him to keep him apprised. He's been my confidant ever since he had the safe house built. He's anchored me more than once. And he knows about Aria, and how badly we've fallen.

"When?" I ask and have to clear my throat after.

"He'll be here tonight, although he's going to his estate and the safe house first to see the damage."

A grunt leaves me before I ask, "He hasn't seen the extent of the damage yet, has he?"

I didn't want to believe it hurt as much as it did when he left. Over time the pain eased. But I can't deny that the memory of him leaving and then not coming back for so long fucking kills me. He was family. He still is.

"Not yet," Jase answers evenly and then adds, "Chloe isn't coming for a while."

"That's understandable," I say absently. Deep in the back of my mind, I always knew he stayed away because of three reasons:

Chloe never wanted to be here.

Romano would have him killed if he still had the power to do so.

Marcus.

When Marcus approaches people, they tend to do his bidding and then move far, far away. My brothers and I are the only ones who seem to have defied that pattern.

It's quiet as the wood splits in the roaring fire and specks of ash fly in the heated air.

"You said there were two reasons?" I remind Jase, waiting on the other reason we shouldn't destroy what's left of Talvery.

"Her father retreated," he tells me, still running his fingers along the blade as he leans back in the chair. He's simply waiting for war. I'm the reason my brothers were pulled into this life, and I fucking hate myself for it.

I hate that he refers to Talvery as "her father" just as much.

"He has to leave eventually. He can't hide forever."

"Until he does, we wait?" Jase asks and I can only nod. Every day this war lasts is a day longer that I have Aria so close, yet unreachable.

"You don't often come to me for advice," Jase comments and I don't respond for a moment.

"I'm tired," I tell him honestly, but I don't tell him everything else. How all I can think about is what I'll be when she leaves me. I'll be the shell of a man waiting to die, the way Jase is waiting for this war.

His gaze burns into me, but he doesn't press me for more. Maybe he already knows.

"Talvery called as well."

My head whips to his and my brows pinch together in both shock and anger at his admission. "When? Why didn't-"

"Just now, before you came in." I try to interrupt him, pissed off that I wasn't told, but Jase continues, "He only wanted to know one thing and then he hung up."

"And you told him what he wanted to know?" My blunt fingernails dig into the soft leather of the armrest.

"He wanted to know if Aria was still alive. If she was okay." He speaks evenly, staring into the fire before looking at me when I ask, "What did you tell him?"

"The truth."

I have to bite my tongue when I nearly ask him what truth he told Talvery. Because I know she's not okay. There's nothing about either of us that's okay.

Chapter 7

Aria

I'll never forget the first fight I had with Nikolai. As I sit in my hideaway room, staring at the beautiful wallpaper in front of me with a blank canvas at my feet and a stick of unused chalk in my hand, I remember how I screamed at him and how he screamed back at me.

It was a quarrel of young love. But it was also the beginning of the end and we both knew it.

He'd taught me to shoot that day, letting me fire his gun. He was only seventeen and I was sixteen. I'd begged him to let me fire it. I wanted to know what it felt like and he told me he shouldn't, and that I would never need to know anyway.

I can't explain how angry it made me, but it didn't matter, because he moved behind me as we stood in front of the forest behind my home. His chest pressed against my back and his hands held mine as he taught me how to fire it.

The gun kicked back, but he held it steady in my hands. I remember the heat that spread through me when he asked me how it felt, whispering the question in my ear. We'd been seeing each other late at night, nearly every night for a while.

I knew he cared for me, but he hadn't said those three words to me that I'd confessed to him.

I peeked over my shoulder, and his lips were right there, so close to mine. I stared at them for a moment and thank God I did, because that's the moment my father stormed out of the house.

I tore myself away from Nikolai before he even saw my father.

That night we didn't fight over the gun, or whether or not I should learn how to fire one. We fought because he wanted to end what we had. He said my father would never allow it.

We fought because I wanted to run away with him, but Nikolai refused. Deciding it was better to stay where we were and to stop seeing each other, rather than to take the risk to leave and keep what we had.

He didn't want to be seen with me again, and that's why I screamed. He was all I had, and he knew it. **It hurt me deeply, although I understood why he didn't want my father to find out. The second I showed him my pain, he took it away.**

Nikolai kissed it away and said he would make it better.

That he was doing it all for me, and one day I'd see. It took time for me to get used to not having him. And every time I cried, every time I needed him, if only for a moment, he came to me.

He never told me he loved me until after I'd gotten over what we had and only considered him a friend. But I knew he did before he told me. Because when you love someone, you can't stand to see them in pain.

Carter's not like that, though. He's not a man to soothe or be soothed. He's the type who puts his thumb inside of a raw gunshot wound and pushes harder. That's the kind of man Carter is.

There's no kissing away my pain with Carter. He wants me to live in it, because he lives in his. To stand by his side means to revel in the agony, and more so, to rule in it.

The knock at my door startles me. It's soft and although I wish it were Carter on the other side, I already know it's not.

Carter's not the type to knock so gently, either.

"Yes?" I call out from behind the closed door.

"It's me." Addison's voice carries through the door and I have to take a steadying breath before I can answer her.

My eyes are tired and burn from lack of sleep as she walks in.

"How did you know I was here?" I ask her and only then do I hear how hoarse my voice is.

As I sit up on my pile of pillows and look around, I realize how pathetic this looks. How pathetic *I* look.

"Daniel told me," she says softly, with a smile that doesn't quite reach her eyes. She looks around awkwardly for only a brief second before coming to sit with me on my makeshift bed.

I want to tell her that I'm happy for her, for what I overheard. I want to hug her and confide in her that I already know the good news, although it was an accident. I want to do many things, but Addison came with a purpose and she doesn't give me a chance to speak first.

I'm grateful for that because seeing her makes me anxious and awkward, given the circumstances.

"When I first moved here... well," she pauses and clears her throat, then continues, "close to here, when I moved to Crescent Hills, I had no one."

I pull my legs into my chest and lean my back against the wall as I watch her sit cross-legged. There's a small pile of plush throw blankets folded next to me and she takes the palest pink one, a soft chenille, and pulls the blanket up around her.

"I know what that's like," I tell her and she shakes her head no.

"I was an orphan," she tells me with her voice cracking and I'm taken aback.

"I had no idea."

"I don't look like an orphan?" she raises her brow and jokes, but the accompanying small laugh is sad. "I don't talk much about it, you know?" I nod as she talks, and I try to imagine what that was like.

"Anyway, I moved between a few different families and

the one here was okay; it wasn't any better than the others in a lot of ways. They didn't care about me, they just got paid to keep me alive, you know?" Addison chews on her bottom lip for a moment and I can't help but wonder why she's telling me all this. She takes in a heavy breath and looks me dead in the eye. "I stayed because of Tyler."

"Tyler?" A freezing sensation sweeps across my skin at hearing his name. It feels as if I know the Cross brother who died. I've dreamed of him, and the words he gave Addison in her dream haven't left me.

"All of us grew up poor, and so he didn't judge me, not like the other kids at school. His father was an alcoholic, and his brothers were... well, they did what they had to in order to survive. And it scared me sometimes. But he loved me, and I loved him in a lot of ways. I also realized I loved his brother—I loved Daniel more, even if we were nothing back then. I hardly spoke to Daniel at the time." Tears cloud her vision and she brushes them away. "The Cross boys, they protected me, they looked out for me in a way no one had. Including Carter." She lets the tears fall and sniffles before telling me, "I swear to you, there's so much good in there."

She licks her lower lip, gathering the tear that lingers there and it's then I realize she thinks I'm not okay because I want to leave. Because I don't love Carter.

"I know there is," I tell her and she waits for more. For the "but" that isn't going to come from me. "I love him and I love this family." Emotions spill from me, emotions I wish I could bury deep down inside until I can't feel them anymore. "I want to be a part of this family more than you could ever know."

She tilts her head and gives me a look, and I actually crack a smile. "Well, maybe you do know." I sniff and look at the ceiling to keep from tearing up at the thought of being a part of this family, a family who has protected me and has loved me. Even if they are ... the men they are.

"So you do love him?" she asks and reaches out to me, laying a hand on my knee. "You forgive him?"

I nod my head, knowing it's true. Both statements are so true.

"He doesn't forgive me." I tell her the truth that burns a hole in my chest. I have to reach into the pocket of the sleepshirt so I can pull out a few of the loose pearls from the necklace I used to wear. The beads click together softly in my hand as I tell her, "He doesn't trust me and he's not going to show any mercy, not to me or to anyone."

"I wanted to come in here and tell you something. Something that's scaring me, Aria." Addison's voice drops and her eyes darken with an intensity I haven't seen from her before.

"Go ahead," I tell her in a whisper, feeling the temperature of my blood drop. She rubs her palms on her jeans as she breathes out slowly.

"I went to Tyler's grave." Tears gather in her eyes the same way clouds do as a storm threatens, slowly and with an impending necessity. "There were so many forget-me-nots." She looks past me, to the window that's covered in beautiful linens, yet locked and will never open. I doubt she knows that little fact though. Her gaze stays there as she tells me, "I brought two packets of seeds with me before I left, and I scattered them all around his grave." Her eyes drift to mine. "It's nothing but a field of blue and white now," she tells me and a chill flows down my spine. An odd sense of déjà vu pricks its way deeper into my bones.

She lets out a steadying breath and shakes her head gently. "I've been dreaming of him since we came back. It's the same dream, Aria."

I remember a dream that's come and gone since I first got here. Since the first week I was locked in the cell in this place, but it's not what she describes.

"Tyler keeps telling me to remind you. Hold him tight. Don't let go... or else he'll die."

In the depths of my being, I know Carter needs someone to love him and someone he can love in return. He's a man in pain, a beast trapped in a castle of his own making. I'm just not convinced that I can be that woman.

Or that he'll let me close enough to be that woman.

"I know," I tell her truthfully. "But it's not all up to me."

"Try," she begs me. "Please, just try to hold on to him."

I swallow my heart, which has traveled all the way up to my throat, and only nod. She has no idea how much I wish I could.

Chapter 8

Carter

Last night she stayed in her room. The one I'm not supposed to go in. I sat by the door and listened to her cry softly. I don't know how much more of this I can take.

My thumb taps on the desk as I stare at the box. She fixed it. She did it. Not me. She didn't ask, and she doesn't know what it does to me. Part of me wants to rip it out. The other part is hoping it means something. Something beyond what I'm capable of controlling.

Knock, knock. The gentle rap at the door disturbs my thoughts. It's early. I've already met with Aden and Jase. We know where every enemy and ally is, and what they're planning. There's nothing to do but wait for Romano to lay Talvery to rest. He'll lose men doing it, but my side has lost enough. And

I informed him of exactly that. His options are limited.

Knock, knock. She knocks again and I have to clear my throat, feeling the roughness at the back as I straighten in my chair and call for her to come in.

The door opens slowly, revealing Aria to me with sleep still in her eyes. Her hair flows down her bare back in waves, and the only thing she's wearing is a thin, black silk nightie with the white pearls draped down her breasts. My cock instantly hardens as she takes a single careful step in, quietly walking on the balls of her feet until she turns and shuts the door with her back to me.

"You look... breathtaking," I say, the words falling from my lips.

Her head turns first, bringing with it the sway of her hips, the gentle swing of her hair around her shoulders and those beautiful eyes that toy with my emotions. Her lips tip up, pulling into a feminine smile as a blush rises up her chest and climbs all the way to her temple. With her head tilted down, she peeks up at me through her lashes, brushing a stray lock from her face and murmurs, "That seems fitting ... since you leave me breathless."

She takes deliberate but slow steps, so I know right where she's headed as she rounds the desk. I don't know why I turn off the monitors, shut my laptop and scoot the chair back, spreading my legs so she can easily climb into my lap. As she adjusts, her small hand slips to my groin and a muffled groan escapes my throat, rumbling my chest. Aria's eyes light with a playfulness, but also so much more. Her eyes always give me more than I deserve.

"I miss you," she whispers as her ass presses against my cock and she lies heavily against my chest. Her hair tickles my neck until she rests her cheek on my shoulder, and lazily presses a small kiss to my throat.

I have a small moment, a split second where I wonder if this is real or a dream. The tension is gone; the thoughts of what will come don't exist in this moment. She simply wants me, and I her. As her nails gently run down my throat, playing among the overgrown stubble, she swallows thickly and I have to wonder if the same thought has hit her as I see pain grow in her expression in the reflection on the black monitor in front of me.

"I didn't think you would come to me," I tell her quietly, and pluck at one of the pearls of her necklace, rolling it between my thumb and forefinger. She nuzzles against my shoulder and whispers in a sultry voice, "I thought you knew me better than that, Mr. Cross." The rough chuckle I give her in return shakes my chest, and along with it, her. Her breasts press against my chest, and I feel her nipples harden from the slight movement.

"I love you," she whispers and kisses my neck again, softer this time, leaving a touch of wetness behind. **There's nothing that could stop me from loving you. I tried. I can't stop,"** she tells me softly, lifting her head to look me in the eyes.

Instead of answering her, I cup her pussy in my lap, pressing my fingers against the thin silk that separates my hand from her hot entrance. She's damp immediately. Wet and hot for me.

As she reaches up to hold on to my shoulders instinctively, I maneuver my fingers around the fabric and press them inside of her. Her back arches and her breasts come closer to my face. I bend down just enough to gently nip the hardened peak of one nipple through the thin fabric, leaving a mark on her nightie.

She squeals in my embrace, jolting slightly, but she doesn't let go of me, she only clings tighter, her nails pressing deeper into my skin through the dress shirt.

"I want you," I breathe against her slender neck as I thrust my fingers in and out of her, moving some of the wetness up and down her cunt and then to her backside, around her tight hole. I need to make the other night right and fuck her there the way she needs.

"I love you," she tells me again in a strangled moan as I unzip my pants and reposition her to straddle me.

Again I don't say it back, and instead I crash my lips to hers, pressing them as deeply as I can as I shove my dick inside of her as swiftly as possible. With both of my hands on her shoulders, my forearms supporting her back, I slam her down, forcing her to scream into my kiss with an ecstasy

I love to give her.

This I can give her. As much as she needs.

She's so fucking tight. Feeling her squeeze my cock with every thrust is something I don't deserve.

Her nails dig into my shoulders and she moans with each upward thrust. The soft sounds are short and come in muted gasps, urging me to push her higher and higher.

The air is hot but my skin is hotter as I feel her tighten around me. I'm close, but I don't want to get off. I don't want to take from her any more than I already have.

I can't breathe as I pound into her with a primal need to force the pleasure to rip through her, but she doesn't let go. She isn't breathing either as her head lolls back, her teeth digging into her bottom lip.

She's watching me as I watch her. With each slam of my hips I want to see her light up with unrelenting pleasure, but she shakes her head gently, barely able to speak as she whispers, "Not without you."

My grip on the flesh of her hip tightens, the threat of her holding back enraging a side of me. A part of my soul buried deep inside that wants nothing more than to give her everything.

With the back of my arm sweeping across the desk, I clear a spot for her, letting everything else crash to the floor so I can move her to lay flat on the desk. The laptop stays to one side, but the phone, the papers and journal with all the numbers, my cell—all that shit clatters to the floor. Her ass is hanging off the desk and my cock is still buried deep inside of her.

I'll make her cum. She won't refuse me.

I take a second, only a single fucking second to wrap her leg higher around my hip so I have the perfect angle to slam myself deep inside of her until she can't hold on any longer. So she'll shatter beneath me like I need her to. But in that second, her eyes widen and she reaches for me, her hand grabbing my shirt and fisting it as she leans up, her shoulders lifting off the desk. As she swallows, I see the plea in her eyes, and how tense her neck becomes.

"Please," she begs me as I hammer myself inside of her, forcing her head to be thrown back as her neck and back both threaten to arch. Even with my ruthless pace, she screams out for me to cum with her, to fall from the highest high and get lost in pieces beneath the world and the reality that plagues us.

"Carter," she moans my name and I cave. I pick up my pace and feel the tingle at the base of my spine. My toes curl and I let them.

As much as I know this won't last, I can't deny her. I won't do it. I love her too much, and that will be my downfall.

Chapter 9

Aria

It's a mix of him not saying he loves me, even though I know he does, and the way he leaves me after sex.

He left me panting and reeling on his desk, my nightgown torn and the pearls wrapped around me so tightly, I felt like they were holding me down. I was a mess, destroyed by him. And he left to clean up, taking his time without me to gather up his own pieces. Every second felt raw. Every moment another bit of reality intruded on the moment.

It reminds me of the time we had in his bathroom when I realized I'd missed my birthday and never went to see my mother. It feels like so long ago when we fought and fucked on the tiled floor. And when he stood, with his back to me and the look of regret clearly written on his face... I'll never forget the way it felt. And that's exactly what it feels like now.

Hold on to him, a voice whispers as the emotions try to strangle my throat. *Hold on to him.*

"I'm trying," I whisper.

"What?" Carter asks and I swallow the dry words, propping myself up on his desk even though I can feel moisture between my legs. I have to wad up the bottom of the nightgown, the bit that should cover my legs, and press it against myself to keep from making a mess. Carter only comes to help me down then. And only to help me down. The moment the balls of my feet hit the hardwood floors, he lets go of me.

I need someone to hold me too. My voice is weak as I answer him, "Nothing." The moment is broken and I feel it inside of me. The sharp edges of it dig into my chest and let the real world find its way back into my head.

Carter's gaze is like fire, burning into the side of my face as I turn away from him, the way he did to me just a moment ago.

"I need to go change." I offer up the excuse and then hate myself for it. I hate that I can pretend in the least that I'm all right.

My hair tickles my upper back as I turn to stare back at the man I love, the man whose love will kill me. With a shiver running down my shoulders and the coolness of his office replacing the much-needed heat I felt a minute ago, I tell him the truth. "It feels like you regret it almost every time you touch me now."

I have to swallow thickly after letting the words out. It is almost every time, isn't it? Each time since the safe house… he never came, not until now.

It's a slow change in his expression, as the slight concern morphs to indifference. To the mask he always wears. "Do you regret this?" I ask him. Before he can even answer, I push out more of the raw truth, saying, "I don't want to feel like this afterward. I don't want to feel…" I trail off as my hand reaches up to my chest and my fingers tangle around the strand of pearls, not knowing what the words are that accurately portray what I feel.

I feel like I lose him more and more when he does this after. But when I'm with him, truly with him, I'm whole. "I want you back." I whisper the words in a ragged voice drenched in despair.

"This isn't going to last." Those are the only words Carter gives me, but his expression says more. His steady gaze belies the hollow depths of his pain. Looking closer, the softness around his eyes shows just how tired he is, how vulnerable, even.

It's only then that tears prick, but still, I hold them back. Sorrow will do nothing for us. It only eats at the precious time we have left.

"Stop." I can only give him a single word before I have to take a steadying breath. I can feel myself breaking, but I won't. He must see it, but he doesn't come to me. He doesn't try to comfort me and I have to reach behind me, gripping the edge of the desk to brace myself.

"You said it yourself." Carter starts to give my own words back to me, and I have to look away from him, staring at the massive windows although I don't see anything at all. "You said you'd never forgive me, and we both know it's the truth and what I deserve."

With my fingers wrapping tight around the pearls, I speak calmly and aimlessly, "Such a reasonable gesture then, to pull away from me and not fight for me." On the last word, I turn to look at him. "Just end it then, send me back?"

Although it's a false threat, a cold chill creeps up my body. It slows everything—my breath, my pulse.

A tic in Carter's jaw starts to spasm as he turns away from me, leaning his hips against the desk and bracing himself on it as I am to look out toward the windows with me.

"The moment I heard your voice, I knew once I had you, I'd never let you go." His voice is low and full of solace. Inside I'm reeling with the ticking time bomb of the truth he doesn't know.

"Which moment?" I ask him.

I can't look at him, knowing what's about to spill from my lips. The revelation that could change everything. If ever there was a time to confess what I've been hiding, it's now, when there's nothing left to hold us together.

"When your father let me go. He let me live, and it's only because you called out."

"It wasn't me," I blurt out, and the words are dead on my lips, completely at odds with the emotion in his. I have to clear my throat and repeat my words when he says nothing at all. "I never knocked at the door. It wasn't me."

"I heard your voice," Carter starts to speak and even takes a half step closer to me, but I cut him off, and stare into his eyes as I confess.

"It wasn't me. I never went to that side of the house." My head shakes as my voice goes hoarse and I have to pause and swallow. My mother died on the floor directly above where my father worked. I never wanted to go back to that side of the house ever again after it happened. "I would have never told my father I needed him. I would have never interrupted his work." My heart clenches with unbearable pain at the look in Carter's eyes. "More than that, my father wouldn't have stopped what he was doing for me," I tell him a truth that causes the small part of me that still craves more love from my father to twist in pain. "It wasn't me you heard."

"You're lying," Carter speaks but there's no conviction.

"You know I don't need to lie to you." With a deep breath in and then a desperate one out, I tell him, "I love you, but if you only want me here because you wanted the girl who saved your life," bastard tears gather in my eyes but I refuse to let them fall as I swallow and continue, "if you only wanted some girl you've dreamed about..."

I can't continue as Carter's eyes narrow at me and his grip tightens on the desk behind him.

"I didn't want to tell you because I thought if you knew, you wouldn't want me anymore." A single tear falls, and I ignore it. "If you only wanted me because of that night, because you thought it was me, then let me leave." When I lick my dry lips, I taste the salt of more tears. Tears I refuse to acknowledge.

"It was never supposed to be me," I whisper as I wipe under my burning eyes and gaze at the bookshelf behind him. His own gaze is unreadable and unforgiving; the mask has slipped back into place.

"I don't believe you," he says and Carter's voice is low and threatening. With the cold air settling against my bare skin, I feel more exposed in this moment than I have in so long. "I know your voice. It was you."

My heart flickers as Carter moves a half step closer, his gaze sizing me up like when I was first in the cell.

"I'm not lying, Carter. It was never supposed to be me."

"I just don't know why you're lying." Carter continues as if I haven't exposed a truth that ruins everything he thought about me, every piece he both hated and loved before he even saw me.

"Stop calling me a liar." A small flame ignites inside of me as he stalks closer, invading my space and towering over me.

My voice is firm, bordering on hard.

I can feel my eyes narrowing on his as he approaches so close I can feel the heat from his skin. The flames lick between us as he smirks at me, letting his gaze roam up and down my body.

"What did you think telling me that would accomplish?" he questions me. It's a fucking interrogation.

Rage burns in my blood. I have to quickly take in a deep breath to keep from snapping.

"I wanted to share something with you that would change things. Something that would sway the position you hold on how we've always been enemies and-"

He cuts me off and rebuts in a casual tone, "But our families have always been enemies."

His gaze is ever assessing. I'm the enemy in this moment. I'm a liar in his eyes.

"You're a fool to think I'd lie to you." My response comes with more pain than I imagined it would.

The smile that graces his lips doesn't hide his hurt. "Am I?"

"I'm not a liar." My hands clench at my sides and the emotions that crept up before crash into me suddenly, like rough waves at the shore. "And this was a mistake." I don't know if I mean telling him he's mistaken, not running when I could... or falling in love with him to begin with. Maybe all of it.

"It was all a mistake," I whisper to myself before looking

back at Carter. At a version of him that's guarded and impenetrable while all I am is vulnerable to him. "I know that now." The realization is sobering.

I meet his gaze as I tell him, "I'm not who you think I am. I'm Aria Talvery and this was never supposed to happen."

With one of his palms braced on the desk, he lowers his gaze until we're eye to eye and his lips are close to mine. So close, and that side of me that wants nothing more than his affection begs me to take them with my own and silence whatever words he dares to speak. But I don't.

"You may be a Talvery, but you're on the wrong territory, little songbird." Backing away slightly, he searches for something in my expression before adding, "And even if you hate me, I won't be letting you go."

Chapter 10

Carter

It wasn't her?

The fuck it wasn't her.

It's all I can think about as I lead her back to the bedroom. The sounds of our footsteps are heavy, but not as heavy as the beating of my pulse.

I know that night, I know her voice. That night, that moment even, changed my life forever. I know every detail. The cadence of her words. I've dreamed of them and been consumed by that moment for years.

The bedroom door closes with a resounding click as I walk to the dresser, where a new glass and bottle of whiskey wait for me.

I go through the motions, barely listening to her undressing and moving through drawers as I try to calm down.

It's an impossible task. Every second, the anger rises.

How dare she lie to me. How dare she look me in the eyes and deny something that led me down a path of violence and self-hate. How fucking dare she do that, yet claim to love me.

I've never hated how capable she is of affecting me more than I do in this moment.

I'll never tell her how much it hurts to hear her deny it. I refuse to let her know. I'll be damned if I ever give her that truth and that power.

As I breathe, the amber liquid flows between the cubes of ice. My grip on the tumbler is loose as I swirl it, but it's no use. I have no appetite for liquor tonight.

I want to punish her. It's all I can think about.

I've handled everything wrong because I've underestimated her, but now that she's shown her cards and revealed what lows she's willing to go to, I won't make that mistake again.

She was right. I should have clipped her wings.

"I don't know why you can't believe me," Aria speaks softly, so softly the rustling of the covers almost drowns out her words as she climbs into bed. Glancing over my shoulder, I watch as she pulls them up closer to her throat and looks back at me the way she always should have, as if I'm the enemy.

I bite down on my tongue to keep from replying as I breathe in through my nose heavily. I don't know why she'd lie about it. What motive is behind her lies?

My shoulders tense as I lean down to grab what's inside the top drawer of my dresser. The sound of it opening is ominous. The metal is cold in my hand as the cuffs clink together. While I walk to her, I think about how to cuff her, but the thought of touching her right now is dangerous. So fucking dangerous.

She casts a spell over me each and every time my skin touches her. I can't risk it.

I toss them on the bed as the thought hits me. "Cuff your left hand to the bedpost," I command her as I drag the chair in the corner of the room toward the bed, closer to her.

With my back to her, I wonder if she'll even obey me until the telltale snap of the closure echoes in the bedroom.

Only then do I breathe and sink down into the chair. I have her, and she's not going anywhere.

The light from the moon shines down on her soft skin in a way that makes my chest ache. She's so fucking beautiful. She brushes her chestnut locks away from her face and stares expectantly at me before resting back against the headboard.

"Are you just going to keep me here until the war is over and I hate you forever?" she asks when I don't say anything. Her voice is flat, but she can't hide the pain in her eyes. She can't hide that from me. Not when I've seen the raw agony the cell brought her, the torment killing Stephan gave her, and the sorrow loving me has stained into those gorgeous hazel eyes.

"That's not a bad idea," I remark, not hiding the exhaustion from my voice.

The huff that leaves her lips is humorless. She tries to get comfortable, but she's cuffed herself too high on the post. The cuff is between the middle and top rung, instead of at the bottom. She can reach the nightstand, where a bottle of wine and a glass from earlier lay, along with her cell phone. At least she can reach those, but nothing else is at her disposal.

Agitation quickly shows in her pursed lips as she props a pillow under her arm. Letting out a sigh, I lean forward, resting my elbows on my knees and stare her down. I wait for her to look at me to ask her, "Why lie?"

Fire smolders in her gaze as she pushes out the words, "It wasn't me."

Tick, tick. It's not the clock, it's the steady beat of my heart, on edge and wanting to know why she'd try to hurt me like she is.

"I have all the time in the world," I tell her and lean back. As I swallow, I realize how much it kills me, the very idea that it was someone else. "It was you," I say, hardening my voice, refusing to entertain the thought the voice that saved me belonged to another. I know it was Aria. Deep in my bones, I know it was her.

"I'm sorry, Carter." Aria's whisper is pained. She scoots closer to me on the bed and I watch as the cuff keeps her away from me. Fuck, I'm a goddamn wreck and she can see.

She could always see me though. Something about her

simply knows who I am. Her soul knows mine.

"I didn't want to tell you," she whispers and I'm taken back to that night, to the pain, to the desperation to die.

"I wanted to die and you saved me," I tell her, knowing how true it is. It was her voice that called out to me as I felt the cold hand of death pull me closer to the ground. Not to a white light and salvation, but down to the dirty concrete floor. And I prayed for it to happen. I coveted nothing less than death to come to me and take the pain away. The torture I endured had destroyed any chance of peace and happiness a boy like me could ever have.

"I'm sorry," is again all she can say as emotion wells in my chest and then higher, up my throat.

"You're not," I speak through clenched teeth and hold on to the fact that she's lying. I know the voice that saved me. "You're a liar."

As Aria tries to wipe away her tears that have slid down her flushed cheeks, she brings her left hand up, only to have it held back by the cuff.

"And you'll stay right there until I'm done doing what I have to do." Standing abruptly, I watch her eyes widen. "You can stay there. Right there where you belong." My words are hollow, but the threat is real. I won't give her up so easily. If she thought lying to me would give her freedom from me, she thought wrong.

"Carter," Aria calls out and moves on the bed, the sheets

falling around her body in a messy puddle, but her left arm is restrained behind her. Frustration joins the desperation in her eyes.

Her right hand moves to her left as if she could pry it free as I stalk to the door. "Carter!" She yells out my name to get me to stop as I stand in the doorway. I stare back at my songbird, naked on her knees in my bed, and chained to it willingly. A dull pink mark still shows on her breast from where I touched her earlier, right beneath the pearls that sway slightly down her front. She's a beautiful fucking vision. Beautiful, but wretched with sadness.

"Don't leave me here," she demands, as if she could, and then swallows visibly.

"You're not in a position to give the commands," is all I give her. I'm only able to take half a step out of the room before the shattering sound of glass at my right is accompanied by wetness along the right side of my cheek, my jaw, my neck and down my shirt. The dark red liquid seeps into my white dress shirt and I stare at the blotches, watching them spread over the fabric before looking back at Aria. The cracked bottle is in pieces at my feet, and there's a small dent in the drywall. It's surrounded by streaks of burgundy that are dripping down to the floor.

My heart races in my chest from shock, but also anger.

"Now you can't hide at the bottom of it." My words are spit with venom as control slips from me.

"Fuck you! I hate you!"

She screams it like she truly means it. Like her hate is the only thing keeping her alive, and I know that's what it is. I've been there. I hated her before she even knew my name.

"I knew you did. I know you hate me. It doesn't change that you're mine." I can't hide the lack of control, the unraveling of composure as I stare her down, watching her chest rise and fall with chaotic breathing.

"I won't let you do this to me," she speaks with conviction and the dry laugh that erupts from my lips is dark and genuine as I grip the doorknob to keep from approaching her.

"Fuck you!" she sneers as she rips her arm away from the bedpost. Not tugging, but yanking her wrist against the cuff. Pain echoes in her face and in the shriek that tears up her throat. My heart slams in my chest as I watch her do it again. And again. My body temperature drops and for a second I don't believe it. She wrenches her body away until a horrid scream comes from her lips. Tears stream down her face as her arm lays limp, and her wrist, still cuffed, is red and raw with cuts from the metal.

"Fuck you," she cries, her words low and full of suffering. She rips her arm away again, although this time she can only use the weight of her body and the action is done without conviction.

Fuck.

I'm too fucking weak for her. Her agony destroys any

rational thought I have. I can't get to her quick enough, although I'm not thinking logically and I don't have the key. In an attempt to help, I grip her as gently as I can to push her back against the headboard to loosen the tension of the cuff, but Aria's hate is stronger than her reason.

Even with a dislocated shoulder, she shoves me with her uninjured hand. "Stay away," she screams at me with tears still falling freely. "Get away!" It's only when she tries to push me again that her body refuses to obey and she clutches at her shoulder.

"Aria," I start to say, ready to plead with her to be reasonable and let me help.

"I meant it, I hate you!" Her confession is sobering. Her face is red as she swallows down the pain and stares me straight in the eye. "You wanted me to be like this? To chain me up and make me pay? You can't go back. That's your thing, right?" She pauses for a moment to breathe and then backs up against the headboard, holding on to her shoulder and sniffling. "Well, you can't go back." Her breathing's unsteady and she speaks softer. "You did this. You made me hate you." Her face crumples with the last confessions. "This is what you wanted, and now you can have it."

The pain is numbing. It takes a minute and then another for me to even retrieve the key to uncuff her. She doesn't look at me at all while I put her shoulder back into place.

And when she sobs, I want nothing more than to hold

her, but she pushes me away and lies on her side, her back to me and her injured shoulder in the air.

I've never hurt so much in my life.

I remember everything from that night years ago. And even that pain doesn't compare to this.

The whiskey is more than tempting this time and it goes down easy.

Each glass is easier than the last, and each brings the picture of our past to me like the way Aria paints. Each moment seems made up of beautiful strokes on her canvas. She could paint a painful past, yet make you desire to touch it with the masterful way her brush moves when she's creating art.

For the longest time, all I see are the moments we've had together.

The next glass brings out my jealousy. And the thought of sending Nikolai a video of me fucking Aria and showing him how much she loves it.

She brings out a possessive side of me I've never known. She makes me lose my control. She ruins everything, but she's the reason for it all.

She's mine.

That's the only thing that matters.

I would never do it; I'd never let a man like Nikolai see

her cum. He had a chance with her, and he lost it. I fucking refuse to lose her like he did. I won't let it happen.

At the thought, the tumbler slams down on the desk. For a moment, I think I've broken it.

I haven't, but the whiskey is humming in my veins and knowing that, I push the glass away from me.

I get down on my knees, feeling lightheaded as I pick up all the shit I threw down from my desk earlier so I could have her. Placing the last few items where they belong, I let my hand rest where her lower back rested only hours ago. The hard chestnut is bitter cold and nothing like her warmth.

My gaze falls to the polaroid pictures laying haphazardly on top of a stack of papers. Pictures I brought out days and days ago to show Aria. Pictures of the house she says is so familiar. And one of them has my father and mother on the porch.

He loved her. Anyone who looked at them could see it. My father loved her with everything he had.

When she died a slow, slow death, he died with her.

I never learned how to love, only how to survive.

Maybe that's what Aria's been doing. Thinking on the past makes me reach for the tumbler again. The liquid burns as I swallow more down in large gulps and remember how she lay on the sofa in the corner of my office that first time.

She was so tired, but well fed and well fucked. The effects of what I'd done to her were still evident. Her skin lacked color and her ribs still poked through her flesh.

I did this to her. I put her in this position to simply survive.

That day she lay on the sofa, she slept off and on. Each time she woke startled and terrified until I went to her. I calmed her. I took her nightmares away.

Tears prick in the back of my eyes as I struggle to breathe. Yes, I hurt her, but I took it all away. All the pain, all the fear.

I thought it counted for more than it did.

As she slept that first day, I couldn't do a damn thing but watch her and every small movement of her body. I remember every inch of her frame. I've never felt so sickened by who I am like back then.

But I tried to take it all away.

My elbows slam down harder than I wanted on the desk as I rest my forehead in my hands and let out a heavy sigh, burdened by all the sins I've committed against Aria Talvery.

It's too much. Tonight has been too much.

I search the top right drawer for the small vial of sweets, but I don't find it. The papers are scattered by the time I'm done, but I don't care. When I slam it shut, the one below opens and I pull it ajar to find what I'm looking for right on top.

I know the liquor will numb me enough to sleep, but I never sleep long and tonight I need it. With a full vial, I swallow it all and when a moment passes and sleep doesn't come, I grab another vial and take more of the drug.

My legs are heavy as I move to the sofa she slept in and lie in her place.

I don't know if I would take it all back. I don't know how I can ever have her. All I wanted was her, and I still do. I can't help it. All I want is for Aria to be mine.

I hear her shuddering breath first. And when I lift my gaze from the floor beneath the desk to her flushed cheeks and then those gorgeous eyes, I feel a weight lifted from me.

Like the pain doesn't exist anymore. Because she's crawling to me. She's coming to me. My songbird.

"Are you still angry?" I ask and my voice feels rough, as if it's been unused for a long time. I can feel my brow pinch in confusion at the thought, and it's then that I realize I feel cold. So cold.

None of it matters when Aria shakes her head. The messy hair around her face lets me know she's been sleeping here in this room. She was waiting for me to wake up.

"I'm not angry." Her voice is soft as she reaches me, but the tears don't stop. My fingers splay in her hair as I cup my hand behind her head and pull her closer to me. I don't even remember what the fight was about when I touch her. Nothing else matters when I touch her. She clings to me, her hands on my thighs as she lifts up her lips and kisses me.

With her lips to mine, everything feels right again and the pain doesn't exist. Not until I feel the wetness from her tears on my face and she shudders in my grasp, pulling away to whisper, "Please forgive me."

It takes me a moment, the haze of the whiskey dulling my

thoughts as I struggle to remember tonight. How she lied, how she said it wasn't her.

"Why did you lie?" I ask her, but she doesn't answer. She only pleads for me to forgive her.

Her voice is wretched as she says, "You never told me that you did and after so long... please, Carter. Please forgive me."

My head pounds with a pain that comes from drinking too much and it takes me a minute to register what she's said. I ask her, "What do you mean 'after so long?'"

She feels so right in my arms, and neither of us are willing to let go, but I feel so dizzy. So cold and confused. The room tilts suddenly. "Fuck," I say, the word stretched in the air and the room tilts again, as if it's trying to make me fall.

"It's been so long since I've seen you," Aria tells me as she touches her fingertips to my face ever so gently. She sniffles and adds, "Since I've gotten to talk to you."

"I just saw you." It's all I can manage to say, but Aria doesn't seem to hear me.

"I love you so much," she says, and her bottom lip wobbles when her eyes find mine. "Please tell me you forgive me. I need it, Carter." She pulls at my hand, holding it in both of hers and cradling my hand to her chest.

"Stop crying," I tell her, trying to breathe but feeling the air become thinner. It's like I'm suffocating. Something's wrong.

I don't want to take my hand away from her, but I need to reach for my collar. I can't fucking breathe. It's then, when I think about moving my hand, that I feel how cold she is against my knuckles. And how still her chest is. And how pale she is.

"Aria." Her name is whispered, but I don't know if I've said it. The chill seeps into my blood. She's not breathing.

"Carter, no. No," she tells me as if she knows what I'm thinking. "It was supposed to end like this. I could never be in the middle of war. I was always going to be the one to die."

What is she saying? No! I scream but there's no sound that escapes from my mouth. The room is silent, save her plea to me. "It's okay. When it happens... I'm okay dying for you. I just need you to forgive me, please. Forgive me and love me, as I love you. I'll always love you."

The prick at the back of my neck flows down every inch of my skin. The room darkens and I still can't breathe. I can't think. She can't be dead. Aria! I scream again, but it's silent.

"We don't have much time. Please, please, Carter. Forgive me." Her eyes search mine as I scream and it's then she sees my mouth moving but there's no sound.

She yells something at me as the distance between us stretches, but her voice is gone.

Aria! I scream her name, reaching for her and holding on to her cold hands with every ounce of strength I have. Don't leave me! I forgive you! I pray she hears me but all she does is cry as the darkness invades every sense I have.

The gasp that fills my chest sends a pain spiking down my back and I fall off the sofa and onto the hard floor of the office.

I'm sweating and my heart is beating wildly in my chest.

My elbow scrapes against the floor as I struggle to get up fast enough.

"Aria!" I scream out, even though there's no way for her to hear me. "Aria!" It's all I can say as I run to her, to my bedroom and throw the door open to find her small form in bed. It's not enough. I can't swallow, I can't breathe, I can't do anything until I yank the covers back and see her chest rise and fall. She moans a small protest in her sleep from the cold, but even still, I lay my hand against her chest, right where it was moments ago, but there's warmth and the steady beat of her heart.

There's a suffocating lump in my throat at the sight of her. Still alive and still here with me. I fall to my knees beside her before covering her with the sheets again.

She doesn't stir from her sleep, and a glance at the nightstand reveals a bottle of painkillers she must have found in the bathroom. It makes sense, given her arm. She's passed out after taking the last two pills I had. But she's here, and she's alive.

It was only a dream. But it felt so fucking real. I struggle to breathe on the floor beside her and even worse, I struggle to get the vision of her out of my head.

I won't sleep until this is over.

I've never hated myself more. I don't care if she lied. I don't care if those words didn't come from her. I've never loved anything or anyone in this life like I do her, the Aria I know, the woman who I know loves me in return. The girl I took and broke, then placed the splintered pieces back together as best I could.

I won't let her die.

Aria Talvery, my songbird, can't die.

Chapter 11

Aria

There's so much pain when I wake up, I feel sick. Literally sick to my stomach as I roll onto the wrong side, my left side, and a screaming pain shoots down my back and then travels up the front of me.

Seething through my clenched teeth, my eyes open wide as I bolt awake in the late morning and I struggle not to vomit.

I wish I could say I was drunk when I lost my shit last night. That's exactly what I did. I have lost all composure when it comes to this man.

It takes me a long time, longer than it should, to realize I'm alone in the bedroom. I expected to see him on the chair watching me, or in bed. I'm not sure why I expected it. I shouldn't have. He's never here in the morning. But we've never been like this before. So broken and each of us hurting the other.

We aren't throwing stones; we're tipping boulders over a steep cliff while the other lies helplessly in the dirt below.

I chose him. I wanted to be with him, and he's choosing to make me feel so fucking alone. The thin top sheet gathers in my hands as fists form and I struggle to hold back the pain from everything.

Waking up alone hurts more than it ever has before. I don't want to be alone anymore. I don't want to be hurting. I don't want to be the cause of Carter's pain either. And I think that's all I'll ever be. After last night, I don't know how I could ever be anything but a painful reminder to him.

Cradling my sore shoulder, I sit up on the bed and let my legs hang off the side as I test out my arm. It hurts like a bitch, but it's my own damn fault. The deep gouges in my wrist are worse though.

The floor's cold under my bare feet as I make my way to the bathroom in search of more painkillers and something I can use to clean the cuts. I don't find either, but I get ready, thinking about the bathroom located off the foyer. I bet there's some in there.

All the while I brush my teeth, I stare at myself in the mirror. As I brush my hair, my reflection does the same, watching the woman I am. There's not an ounce of happiness. There's nothing but darkness.

I read in some article a while back, that pets start to look like their owners because they learn to mimic their facial expressions. It's the same with adopted children resembling parents who aren't biological. The more time spent with someone, the more you inherit their features.

And as I stare at myself, all I see is the darkness that is Carter. The brewing pain deep inside. It inhabits me in a way I hadn't seen before.

The room is silent as I turn off the water and carefully set my brush on the granite counter.

None of this belongs to me. None of it is mine.

Every piece was a gift, comfort items meant to placate me. With a step back, it's hard to swallow. With a peek up in the mirror, it's hard to withstand the sight.

It's never been more clear to me that I need to leave than in this moment. Carter Cross is a drug I'll never kick. A drug that's seeped into my veins and wrapped its way around every small piece of me.

I'm addicted to what he does to me and he'll just continue to hurt me. He knows how much he hurts me, as do I, and yet here I am.

When I turn my back, it feels like someone else is there, someone behind me. The girl in the mirror maybe. She's watching me and it sends pricks down my neck as I slowly leave the bathroom, too cold and disturbed to dare shut the door.

Even as I dress, slowly and with a searing burn every time

I have to move my left shoulder, I stare at the bathroom as if somewhere deep inside, a part of me is waiting for a person to leave it.

I can't shake this feeling. Not until I leave the bedroom. At least for a moment.

It feels too empty as I walk alone to the foyer bathroom. I'm hollow inside with the wretched truth so clear in my mind.

Leaving someone who hurts you shouldn't feel like this. Like you're losing a part of your soul. As if inside, there's a fissure that's expanding, and as it does, it's damaging whatever it is that makes a person alive. Whatever makes me feel is being scarred with every step I take.

Because the closer I get to the front door, the more I want to leave and never look back.

I could never, even for a second, look behind. I can already imagine his face and the way he'd look at me if I left him.

I can *feel* his pain.

As I round the corner, I'm careful to contain my emotions so I don't break down again.

With a quick intake of air, I stiffen the moment I look ahead of me, straight at the open bathroom door.

Even my heart stills, not wanting me to be heard or seen.

Addison doesn't see me as she pulls her hair into a ponytail. She's in her head, I know she is. I can practically see the wheels spinning as she walks down the right hall, past the bathroom.

It's only when she's out of sight that I even dare breathe.

I still don't move though. My limbs don't allow it.

How did I let my life come to this? Where I'm afraid to see the only friend I'm able to interact with because ... because why? Because I'm ashamed, and scared, and miserable with who I am and the choices I've made, and I can't tell her any of that... because she's on the side of the enemy.

That fissure deep inside of me, the one destroying everything in its path, rips me wide fucking open as I walk as quietly as I can to the small half bath and close the door.

The click sounds like the loudest thing I've ever heard as I sit down on the toilet and cover my face with my hands.

I feel hot and immediately I have the urge again to vomit as I reach up and my shoulder sends a bolt of pain down my back. *Fuck!*

I bite down on the inside of my cheek so hard, I can taste the metallic tang of blood. It was worth it not to scream though. Still, I want to scream so badly. I want to get all of this out of me.

I'm stronger than this, but it feels like there's something inside of me that's falling apart in a way where I know it will never be whole again.

There's a line in one of my favorite stories from *Alice in Wonderland*, that goes something to the effect of, there's no use to going back to yesterday, you're a different person than you were then.

I hate that line now. I used to love it. I could have lived by that sentiment, feeling purposeful and fulfilled. Right now? The very idea of that quote forces me to jump off the toilet seat so I can hurl what little I have inside of me into the bowl.

It's fucking disgusting. The taste, the smell, the burning feeling. And when I'm done, while I'm washing my mouth out with the running water, I don't feel any better at all.

Deep breaths get me through cleaning it all up. It's when I'm searching under the sink for a new hand towel to replace the one I used to wipe my mouth that I see the box of pregnancy tests.

Addison.

"Oh my god." The words leave me in a whisper and for the first time this morning I smile. It's only a hint of one, but now I have a light that's growing, if dim. She's pregnant. I fall down on my ass and lean against the wall as I hold the box of pregnancy tests and wonder what she's feeling and thinking. She's going to have a baby. And what a wonderful mother she'll be. I know she will.

The light inside of me is quick to fade though as I realize she didn't tell me. But maybe there's nothing to tell. The thick wrapper on the test I pull out crinkles in my hand and I think back to my last period... before all of this started.

The days have faded and with the shot Carter gave me, I never considered any other reason for not getting my period.

I'm constantly tired, irritated and emotional, and now

sick. Sick to my stomach. But sick and tired would also describe anyone in my situation. Still, a heated wave of anxiousness rolls through me until I move to take the test.

Tick.

Tick.

Time passes and my thoughts run wild.

Tick.

Tick.

Time passes as the turmoil and sickness subside, leaving a dust to settle and a clear picture to form.

Tick.

Tick.

I don't know how long I sit there holding the box.

Or how long I wonder if it's worthless. If all of this is worthless.

I don't need a friend. I don't need someone to love me either.

I need to get the fuck out of here.

Chapter 12

Carter

I can't get the sound of her pleading for me to forgive her out of my head. The words are etched inside of me, ricocheting around the walls of every room I enter.

Exactly how her words years ago followed me, but these pleas are haunting in a way I've never felt.

It was too real.

Even though I'm in my desk chair, waiting on my brothers, I can't stop staring at where she was last night. I'm still staring at the spot when the door opens and that's when I glance at the monitor, expecting to see Aria sleeping, but she's already up and getting dressed.

I don't know who's come in, but I start talking anyway. "We need to call the doctor." I let the air in my lungs leave me before seeing Jase and Declan walk in and each take a seat. Jase sits easily in the chair in front of the desk on the right. Declan leaves the one on the left, presumably for Sebastian or Daniel.

Sebastian got in late last night to his place, where he slept, going against what I recommended, and he's on his way here now. I need him here. I need my friend to help me figure out what's wrong with me.

Declan leans against the bookshelf, slipping his phone into his pocket and letting his head fall back against the wooden slat to ask me, "The doctor?"

His brow is pinched and I take a moment to really look at him. He's aged so much in the last few years.

I can hear Daniel's heavy steps sounding down the hall as I nod at Declan, feeling my throat getting tighter even though I attempt to relax and lean back into my chair. "Aria hurt her shoulder last night."

The pain in my chest radiates. "Last night was difficult." I can't look my brothers in the eyes, and Daniel walks in just then. The door closes quietly as I peek back to the sofa I slept on last night and then to Daniel, who asks for the time.

"We have six minutes," Jase answers him and quickly gets back to me and my lost thoughts. "What'd she do?" he asks me.

Shame is bitter. It tastes so fucking bitter.

"Is she all right?" Declan asks, and Daniel is quick to ask what's wrong as he takes the left seat across from my desk.

"Aria hurt her shoulder last night is all. She's fine," I say. It's a lie and with how silent the room is, my brothers know it too. I can't tell them what happened though. I can barely stand to look at myself, knowing what happened last night.

"Five minutes." Jase breaks the silence, lifting his arm to check his watch. The light glints off the shiny metal and I welcome the distraction. I wish I hadn't brought it up at all, but I'm not used to hiding anything from my brothers.

"When we're done, I'll handle that, but this call will hopefully give us something."

"Just so you know, we gave the last case of guns to Romano and pulled everyone."

"So they have everything they wanted?" Daniel clarifies with Jase at the news, and Jase nods.

We've been involved enough, and Talvery doesn't have the men to threaten us anymore.

"Good," Declan remarks, "Let the two of them kill each other."

My grip tightens on the smooth leather of the armrest as I stare at Jase and tell him, "All I want is to keep them all away from here." He nods easily at first, in complete agreement but when he looks back at me, his expression becomes more serious. "No one gets close," I say, and my voice hardens, thinking about keeping Aria safe. I won't let her die.

"Of course," Jase tells me, his gaze searching my face for what's changed since I last spoke to him yesterday about pulling everyone. I know I'm still shaken and out of everyone, I know Jase can tell something's off.

I'm saved from his inquisition as the door opens, and Sebastian comes in. His hair is longer, his scruff now a short and neatly trimmed beard. His eyes have aged, but the man I once knew like a brother, walks into the office and I can feel the tension start to leave my body almost immediately.

"Sorry I'm late."

"Welcome home," I tell him, meeting his gaze, but my own words are drowned out by those of my brothers. When we were younger, Sebastian was all we had to guide us.

My body's stiff as I make my way around to greet him. Seeing him is bittersweet. Time has passed, and both of us have changed. But in this cruel world we live in where you have to fight to survive, there's nothing like a friend who's been there every time you've needed them.

In Sebastian's case, every time but one, but there's no time to dwell on the past. Again my gaze shifts to the empty sofa as I head back toward my seat.

I'm still so fucking cold, and for a moment I feel like I can't breathe again.

"It's good to see you guys again," Sebastian says and then takes us in one by one.

"I wish things were different," I tell him and no words could speak more truth.

"It's only a little bloodshed," Sebastian offers, smirking

and leaning back against the wall.

"You all right?" he asks me, and he doesn't hide the concern in his question. He never has, and with those words I'm taken back to when I was only a child and all the times he asked me the exact same thing.

"I'm ready for this to be over," I answer him and we share a knowing look.

"I guess it's good that I came then." His answer is firm, but comes out in a way that makes me feel slightly relieved.

I give him as much of a genuine smile as I can as he walks over the spot Aria was in last night and then back to the door. *It was only a dream.* I have to remind myself.

Sebastian asks Declan as he leans against the closed door, "Are you all set?" My brother gives him a nod, and an arrogant smirk in return.

Declan stalks from the bookshelf and walks closer to the desk, his eyes on the telephone seated in the left corner as he says, "Tracers are on and these are new. Even if he's bouncing his signal off multiple towers, or the call cuts off in seconds, I can find him."

My back is stiff with tension... but also the creeping feeling of danger. We're going to hunt down the grim reaper, one of the names Marcus goes by.

"Are you sure?" He nods at Daniel's question and then all of us stare at the phone, preparing to get answers we've waited far too long for as it rings, as if daring Declan to be right.

Ring.

I can feel the desk vibrate and the small shaking movements of the phone as I reach for it.

Lifting the handset up and putting it on speaker, I let Marcus know we're all here.

"The Cross brothers," he speaks. Marcus, the grim reaper, the ghost… whatever name he goes by, he's finally gracing us with a call. My teeth clench when I hear his voice, and my blood goes cold.

His voice has always reminded me of a snake. Not a snake you can easily kill by cutting off its head, but the kind of snake that myths make immortal.

It's the way his words linger in the air and settle into your bones.

"It's been a while," Marcus comments and Daniel's quick to reply, "Not because of our doing."

My left hand raises silently in the air, quieting Daniel although I can see the anger rising inside of him as he's barely grounded in the chair. He knows Marcus has answers, and he's refusing to give them to us.

"I believe our desired outcomes may no longer be aligned, Marcus." My heartbeat quickens, but I keep my voice even and remain calm and in control. "Is that why you've been quietly avoiding us?" I question him.

Silence. For one beat, and then another.

I can feel my brothers watching me, their eyes boring into

me, but I stare at the phone, willing Marcus to answer.

And finally, I'm given a response. "Not necessarily," he answers me and then adds, "You made a change that I didn't necessarily agree with, Cross."

"You'll have to be more clear on which of us you're referring to," I tell him as I rest my elbow on the table and my chin on my fist. My thumb runs along my stubble as I glance at Declan, who's watching the tablet in his hand with an unyielding stare.

"I suppose you're right..." Marcus says and then pauses before adding, "Two of you have in fact, gone off course."

Daniel's eyes meet mine at the same time I look at him.

"What exactly changed that you decided we were no longer allies?" I ask Marcus, feeling hotter and growing irritated. Marcus is an unparalleled force, but he aggravates the fuck out of me with how cautious he is. When I can use him to my advantage, which I have in the past, I think highly of the man. I've both feared and admired him.

But to be on the other side of his temper is ... enraging.

"I needed to make a deal with Nicholas Talvery." Marcus surprises me with a straight answer.

I surmise, "And my interfering was..."

"Unappreciated." Marcus finishes my sentence and I merely nod, my mouth set in a grim, straight line.

"What happened with Addison?" Daniel asks, and Marcus ignores him.

"I want Aria Talvery." Marcus's demand gets a reaction from me that he can't see. My brow raises and a smile wavers against my lips.

"No." I'm surprisingly calm as I answer, "That's not going to happen."

The ever-present ticking of the clock passes in the silence until Marcus responds, "I didn't anticipate your response to be so.... shortsighted."

"Daniel asked you a question," I remind Marcus and watch my brother. "Why was she involved?" I'm not positive that Marcus is behind what happened, but I know that he knows the answer.

"Why did you try to take her?" Daniel's question comes with a raised voice behind clenched teeth and barely contained anger. His inability to keep calm is understandable, but ineffective.

"I didn't. You already know who did."

I barely contain my irritation, watching Daniel come unhinged as Marcus continues to skirt around the one thing he needs to know.

"If we knew, we wouldn't be asking you," I tell Marcus pointedly.

"Who tried to take Addison?" Daniel speaks up with the only question he wants answered. I have so many I could drown in them, but he only has one.

I expect a single name. Or the denial of information

entirely. Instead, Marcus continues to evade the answer, but he also surprises me.

I don't like to be surprised, because it means I'm lacking in information, which means I'm lacking in control.

"The same man who hurt you years ago and started all this." *Years ago*? His words repeat in my head. In the decade since we've taken power, no one has dared to hurt us until recently.

Marcus continues and this time, he places a small clue in his response. "She wouldn't be yours if it hadn't happened."

"If what hadn't happened?" Jase asks, speaking for the first time. And now I'm left wondering if Marcus is referring to Addison or Aria.

"The first hit your family took," Marcus says, giving more information to solve a riddle rather than providing an answer that would be so easy to give.

"You talk in circles and riddles," Daniel sneers and then slams his fist down before raising his voice to tell him, "I just want a name."

"And I just want Aria," Marcus answers, ever calm in a way that makes my blood turn to ice.

My brother looks at me, desperate for information, but before I can respond, Daniel narrows his eyes at the phone and tells Marcus, "If all you're after is Aria, this conversation is useless. We will never give her to you."

The line clicks dead and the moment it does, I stare at Daniel, who won't take his gaze from the silent phone. With his jaw clenched and every emotion written on his face, I feel nothing but sorrow for him. Maybe shame as well. I'm ashamed I brought my brothers into this, and I don't have a way to fix it.

"Years ago?" Sebastian repeats Marcus's words and opens the door as Declan moves to leave, looking pissed off.

"Did it-"

Before Sebastian can even finish his question, Declan's fist slams against the doorframe, splintering it with his rage.

He doesn't speak; he doesn't even slow his pace. Declan's the first to leave and Daniel follows.

"Can I have a minute with Sebastian?" I ask Jase, letting go of my thoughts of figuring out what Marcus was hinting at. With a nod, Jase is gone, leaving only Sebastian and myself.

"Don't let anyone close to this place and only trust us," I tell Sebastian, not wasting a second as he stalks to where Jase was just sitting. With both hands wrapped around the back of the chair, he looks at me closely.

"Are you all right?" he asks me again and the sad smirk comes faster this time.

"No."

"What has to happen?" he asks, and I'm grateful for that question rather than the obvious, *why?*

"She needs to be kept safe. Aria Talvery."

"Because he wants her?" he guesses and I keep my expression still and unwavering, but after a short moment,

I shake my head. "It has nothing to do with Marcus. She simply needs to be kept safe."

His eyes search mine, and I hate his hesitation.

"You know what she means to me," I speak with desperation and hate that I have to say it at all. It was his idea to give Stephan to Aria. Between my brothers and Sebastian, they know all my secrets. Loving Aria isn't a secret anymore, and Sebastian knows it.

"I don't care what happens, as long as you keep her safe. She can't be hurt. In any way."

"So you want me to ... be her guard?" he offers and I hadn't thought of it like that, but I nod, knowing I need someone to watch over Aria.

Sebastian nods and tells me we'll talk more in detail soon before turning and leaving. And that's the end of this very short meeting.

After he leaves, I wish he hadn't. I'm alone in the room with the memories of last night, and riddles I don't know how to begin to solve. The world feels like it's closing in on me, and years of sin are mere seconds from destroying what's left of me.

"I had a thought," Jase speaks and I open my eyes, realizing that I didn't even hear him come back in.

"I need to check on Aria," I tell him, not wanting to deal with more shit. She has to meet Sebastian, and a strange sensation curdles the bit of bile in the pit of my stomach at the thought of what she'll tell him about me.

"Just listen for a minute."

"One minute," I say. I focus on the phone, on the conversation that keeps repeating itself in the back of my mind as Jase tells me we should meet with Nikolai and let Aria see it all. Let her watch as Nikolai shows himself to be the man he is in front of her.

"What if she saw him the way we do?" he suggests and stares at me expectantly.

"I can't even begin to understand why you would think that's a good idea."

"Let Aria see. Let her see you give him the chance to walk away, and show her the side of him she doesn't know about."

"Why-" I almost question my brother's sanity until I realize he thinks I'm fucked up today because of Nikolai. He has no idea what weight I'm carrying today, but his first guess is that it has to do with Aria and Nikolai.

"You think that she'd be all right with him dying then? You're wrong." I don't give him a moment to respond.

"I don't give a fuck about Nikolai, and I've resigned myself to the fact that Aria is going to hate me for what I'm about to do. What she knows and doesn't know is irrelevant."

Defeat crosses Jase's expression when I tell him a truth I wish didn't exist.

"She loved him first, I know that. And she loves me now." I swallow thickly and then tell him, "A part of her will always love him, but a part will always love me too."

"I'm struggling here," Jase says and runs a hand through his hair. "Something's wrong."

How could he not see? How could anyone not understand?

"I don't know how this is supposed to end any other way but with us apart."

There's no way for this to end other than for her to hate me, or for me to die.

"She understands-"

"And I understand she'll hate me when it's over," I cut him off with my rushed words. "What everyone needs to understand is that even if..." I have to pause and take a deep breath, staring past my brother at the closed door as I continue, "Even if she leaves... Even if she decides she can't live with..." I've thought of this ending so many times, but I've never fully accepted it until this moment.

"Even if she doesn't want me anymore when this is all over, I want her protected. I want her safe. Even if she can't live with being my wife, my lover, my ... everything. Even still, I need everyone to know that she's protected and that she'll always be mine."

Chapter 13

Aria

Carter never changed the lock.

It's funny how regret sweeps through me as I open the front door. My hand is heavy with it and as I look over my shoulder, back down the hall, so are my legs. When I put my hand to the scanner, I didn't expect for it to work. I didn't think it would be so effortless.

Saying goodbye is never easy. Especially the kind of goodbye that's final. The kind that hurts to say out loud, but it hurts even more when buried deep down inside.

I only stand in the doorway for a moment before I feel the breeze in the early evening air. I'm surprised no one's running down the hall when I close the door behind me.

Even more surprised when I wrap my arms around myself,

careful with my left shoulder, although it's feeling better now with the pain pills I found in the half bath's medicine cabinet.

The wind brushes my hair from my shoulder, exposing my skin to the cold. Goosebumps flow over my skin as I take each step down, each step farther away from Carter.

Part of me wonders if he's watching. Another part knows that he is.

He won't let me get far. I already know that, but I need to know how far he'll allow before someone will come and scoop me up to take me back to him.

Whether it happens today, or tomorrow, or a week from now, I'll never stop trying to leave. I repeat those words in my head as I take another step.

I don't think of the reasons. There are too many at this point, and only the outcome matters.

I can't stay here any longer. This isn't the life I want. It's never been more clear than it is now.

My pace doesn't slow until I get to a metal gate at the end of the drive. I hadn't seen it before through all the trees, and I guess it was open last time the cars drove through.

I can't imagine they keep anything out but vehicles, because the gaps in the intricate metal are plenty wide enough for a person to pass through.

And I do.

My fingers grip the cold iron and I duck my head as I turn to slip through the bars.

Peering back at the house, I know he's watching and when I turn back to the remaining driveway that carries on for at least a quarter mile and then weaves through a thick forest, I know he's going to stop me soon. The cameras at the top of the gate swivel, following me.

My heart flickers weakly. The stupid thing doesn't understand. It's still filled with hope.

There's no hope though. There never was.

Chapter 14

Carter

Maybe if she's not with me, she won't die for me.

The thought comes and goes quickly, but as I watched her walk down the porch steps, it was there for a moment.

That I could let her go to save her.

She can't die for me, if I'm not with her.

The thought is only a small blip in my consciousness, but it keeps coming back. Even as Sebastian runs into the room to tell me she's out front. I don't have time to question fate and what I've done. I can't leave her unprotected. That's not an option. I won't allow it.

"I know." The words come out even but low, with a threatening menace I can't hide.

"We've got an eye on her." He's catching his breath, his

chest rising and falling with heavy pants, but his demeanor is calm. His words though, are prying. "Does she normally walk out past the gate?" He's careful not to ask outright if she's trying to escape, which is something I'm not used to from him. I can see the change in the way he looks at me. Time's changed many things since the last time we've done something like this together.

It takes a moment, another moment before I can even breathe at the realization. A decade has passed, and I hate what I've become.

I didn't want to be this man. I didn't ask for this life.

As much as I wish I could, I can't go back. My gaze centers on Sebastian, holding the authority I've fucking earned. "Lock her up." Every syllable comes out hard, and each word is accompanied with a slamming in my chest.

She can't die then. She's safe here.

"Everything is barricaded, guarded and armed. No one is getting close and no one is going to hurt her." The words echo in the room and Sebastian is silent. He already knows I'm merely reassuring myself.

"Just snatch her up?" Sebastian asks easily, as if there's nothing at all wrong with what I'm doing. I nod, feeling a knot wind tighter in my stomach, twisting unforgivingly at the fact that she's trying to leave me. Willing to leave me.

"I know she's angry." I try to justify the fact that she's leaving, but I swallow my words. "I'll make it right with her,"

I say as I turn away from Sebastian and move to the window to see how much farther she's gone. "Don't let her get much farther than the gate."

"You think she'll go all the way down the drive?" Jase questions from behind me. There are men lining the estate, past the drive although it's still not safe. I don't bother to turn to him as the sun sets beyond the trees, where it's least protected. The light blue in the sky instantly darkens as the auburn leaves weave patterns with the remaining light.

"Just get her." The knot climbs up my stomach and twists and turns inside of me. It's a pain I haven't felt before.

Last night plays out as I look at myself in the reflection of the window. I love her. I love her completely and without hesitation. But the man I am is one who destroys.

The fact that some part of her loves me, only means she's setting herself up to be ruined. Every piece of her broken... by me.

As I swallow down the thought, my hands move to my pockets and I vow to fix this between us. I don't have another option. I won't let her go.

"You all right?" Jase's voice brings me back to the present and as I turn to him, I look back to the sofa. Empty. Just as the floor is in front of my desk. The visions of last night pass like another blip.

Sebastian's gone, and Jase has taken his place. Time is moving like the flickering images of an old movie reel with some of the frames missing. I don't know how long Sebastian's been gone or when Jase came into my office.

"No," I answer my brother honestly and my next words come out ragged. "I've never been like this. I've never," I pause to pull my hands from my pockets and run them over my face. Staring at the drawer to my desk, I remember taking the sleep aid last night. It's only a drug and it's never affected me like this. It has to be the drug. *The sweets.* The last time I took it was years ago.

"She's just angry," Jase says then looks over his shoulder before shutting the office door and coming to take his seat opposite me.

"I don't want to sit," I tell him with agitation before he can sink into the chair.

I watch his knuckles tighten as he grips the back of the seat. "I want this over. We need to end it." My words come out harder and faster as the desperation to move past this with Aria takes over.

"We're letting Romano-"

"Fuck Romano!" I slam the back of my clenched hand against my chair, needing to feel something other than this pain that's creeping inside of me. Needing to do something other than wait.

"We can't do both, Carter." Jase's voice is calm, but full of reason. He doesn't move from where he is, but his eyes watch me with increased interest. "We can't guard the estate and also attack Talvery's." He finally moves, backing away from the chair although his hands still grip it. "You can't have it both ways."

Time marches on as I consider my brother. The one thing he's always had is an opinion. Constant fucking ideas. Constant pushing. Yet as I lean forward, breathing in to steady myself, he's quiet. He's not pushing either way.

"What would you do?" I ask him, not looking at him, but instead staring at the closed door behind him.

"I can't answer that," he tells me and I fucking hate him for leaving me with nothing. The back of my jaw clenches as I peer down at the screen. She's at the gate.

She's leaving me.

It was never supposed to be me.

Her words from last night, words that wrecked me and caused all of this shit. Those words come back and as I watch her, I believe her.

"She told me," I swallow before finishing my thought, questioning telling Jase any of this but deciding I need to tell someone, "She told me it wasn't her all those years ago."

It takes Jase a moment before his expression registers what I'm talking about. He knows about that night. As well as Declan and Daniel, Sebastian too. That night changed everything. For her to deny being a part of it... I can't fucking stand it.

"Who else could it have been?"

"No one." My answer is immediate and unforgiving,

joined with a similar pain in my throat as it tightens. My eyes close as I think to myself, *how would I know? How could I possibly know if another woman was there?*

"Carter," Jase's voice cuts off the memory of that night. "What happened to her shoulder?"

"I cuffed her to the bed. Well, she did, because I told her to." Jase doesn't waver as I lick my lower lip, hiding the shame. "I told her she could stay there until it was over." My eyes lift and I find his as I explain, "And then she ripped her arm away until it dislocated and I uncuffed her, but she..." I can't even finish.

"She did it to herself?"

"Physically... yes." It feels like a lie on my tongue. I'm the reason it happened. It's my fault.

Jase's nod of understanding is short and then he peers past me to the window. "Well, that explains why she ran."

"She'll always run," I tell him as the knowing defeat gets the better of me.

"Stop lying to yourself." Jase's calm voice catches me off guard. "You love her. I know it. And she loves you. Don't let anything come between you."

Love isn't always enough, I think, but I don't say it out loud. Instead my gaze turns to the floor in front of my desk, last night still reeling in my mind. The image of her lying there comes and goes with the blinking of my eyes. "You need to help me keep her safe." I don't know how I even speak. My body is stiff and my limbs are frozen.

"You're scaring me with the way you've been today." Again Jase's feet and posture shift, but his grip remains stiff, keeping him where he is.

I look back to the sofa while I tell him the one thing that's responsible for how I've been today, "I don't want her to die."

"It's not going to happen." Jase's answer is nothing but confident. I wish last night hadn't stolen that same certainty from me. I almost tell him about the nightmare. About how real it was, and how it's fucking with me.

"Whatever's gotten into your head," he starts to say, the concern etched in Jase's words making me look back to him as he finishes his thought, "get it out."

"I just didn't sleep well." I give him a half truth.

"Well tell Aria you love her, fuck her until she forgets why she's angry and sleep. Both of you need to sleep."

"Is that all I need to do?" I question him to lighten the tension, but it does just the opposite.

"You can start with showing her more respect than you have in the past. More love. Tell her you love her."

"She's not leaving because I don't say it back to her." I scoff at his suggestion.

"I think that's exactly why she's leaving. That, and the fact that you told her what to do." His words register one by one. "I think she would let you destroy everything in her world but you, so long as you showed her how much you loved her and told her often."

I don't know when my brother became the voice of reason, but everything he's saying sinks in deep and slow, numbing the anger, the need to fight. Numbing the guilt and the worries. It all seems to fade at the very thought that I can keep her. That it's possible.

"If she felt the love you have for her, she wouldn't leave. No one would give that up." His dark eyes shine with a memory of something else. Something I know has nothing to do with me, but his next words are exactly what I need to hear at this moment. "She doesn't feel loved, and I know you can make her feel it."

How can she not feel everything I feel for her? How can she not feel *this*?

Just as the question consumes me, the phone rings and it's the same number as before.

Marcus.

Chapter 15

Aria

Maybe a quarter mile.

The driveway to the estate is miles long. Miles. The cast iron streetlights that line it cast a pale yellow glow down the paved road that winds through the woods, and I got maybe a quarter mile from the gate before I heard the gravel kick up as tires moved behind me. Gazing to place where the woods begin, I think maybe they're another quarter mile away.

The car heading toward me isn't driving fast and I merely walk to the side of the road and stand there crossing my arms when I hear it approach. I imagine I look like a petulant child, but it's only because I'm cold. The evening air in the shade is bitter and unforgiving.

My shoulder is numb, and so is all the pain. I'm ready for

it to end. However it comes, I'm prepared for what's next.

The thought makes my throat tighten and that's when the window rolls down. It's Sebastian, not Carter. It takes me a moment to even recognize that it's him. Addison told me about him when we were at his safe house. She showed me a few pictures of Carter and his brothers with Sebastian in them. I know it's him, but that doesn't dampen the disappointment that Carter didn't come himself.

"Carter sent you?" I ask beneath my breath. Hating that I even expected Carter to bother with acquiring me. Of course he wouldn't. With the car idling, I wait for the man to speak.

He's obviously older, but his features are classically handsome. He's the type of man who could get away with whatever he wanted; he could charm you into anything. Even if there is an air of danger that surrounds him.

"Will you do me a favor and get in easy?" he asks me and a handsome smirk shows off his perfect teeth. "I'll do you a favor in return," he offers.

Kicking at the driveway, I let my gaze fall and then feel the chill in the breeze before I ask him, "What's that?"

"I'll drive; we can drive a bit until you calm down?" he offers. "You can tell me why you're upset."

Although he's seemingly kind, I loathe what he just said. "Upset?" I swallow thickly after speaking and Sebastian puts both of his hands up in defense.

"I don't want to make anything worse or step on anyone's

toes, Aria." His voice pleads with me as he adds, "Just help me make this better if I can."

The sky darkens as I wait a moment. Watching this man and finding myself envious of him. He knew Carter. The boy before he turned into what he is now. Curiosity overwhelms any anger with that thought.

My legs move on their own and I find myself climbing into the car. The door shuts with a dull thud, silencing the faint sounds of the forest.

"I'm Aria," I offer him even though he already knows. "I'm sorry we had to meet this way." My manners seem to come back to me as he lets off the brakes and we move forward.

The locks in the car are automatic and they slam down, sounding far louder than they should and reminding me what all of this is for me, a prison.

"I've met people under worse circumstances," he tells me. He keeps his word, driving slowly on the long path. So slow I could walk faster than this, but I'm simply grateful to be heading away from Carter's castle of heartlessness.

"I don't want to go back," I say absently. I don't expect it to make any bit of difference. As the confession leaves me, I stare at the lock on the door, so easily lifted if only I were to reach out.

"You know I have to give you back to him, right?"

My pulse races and then seems to frost over as I remember Daniel offering me an out only days ago. I could have run, I could have accepted Daniel's offer, although who knows if he truly meant it or not.

"I've never seen him like this." Sebastian starts to say something else, but then he shakes his head and waves off the thought. "I don't want to get in between you two," he tells me.

"Everyone else is," I answer flatly and then really look at him until his eyes dart to mine. "Everyone has always been between us." That's the sad truth. If it were only us, there's no question I'd be by his side.

Parts of Sebastian remind me of Eli, or maybe I simply long for someone to confide in, someone who understands and respects the situation the way Eli did. The thought brings a swell of emotion up my chest and I stare out of the window, at the dark green leaves strewn in between the dried-up amber ones.

"Hey." Sebastian's voice brings my focus back to him.

"Have you talked to him today?" The concern on his face seems out of place as he waits for me to answer.

"I just got up, and…" I trail off to swallow the sickness rising up my throat, remembering what happened when I made it to the bathroom. "I haven't." There's nothing left to say. That's the truth of the situation, but I don't bother to voice it.

The silence in the car is awkward. Sebastian asks questions I don't want to answer.

"What's wrong?"

I don't bother to even give him a response to that one.

"Do you like the quiet too?" he asks me after a moment passes with neither of us talking.

"You like the quiet?" I ask him to clarify and he shakes his head no.

"Carter always did."

Again I turn to the window. It's not shocking that the brooding man prefers silence. And the way that little fact tugs at me makes me wish I hadn't climbed into the car.

"Although some days he'd turn up the radio just to numb it all out." He clears his throat and turns the car around. As he's making the three-point turn to head back to the estate he tells me, "When he'd stay with me, back when his mom was sick, he always wanted it to be quiet. He used to say the quiet was his safe place, but then again, he grew up with four brothers and the only time it was quiet was when he wasn't home… so…" He shrugs.

"What was he like back then?"

Sebastian regards me for a second and slows down as we near the estate.

"Stubborn, ambitious," he answers me and then says, "loyal to a fault."

He stops in front of the gate and I ask him to go around just one more time. My hands feel clammy as my gaze flicks to the lock and then back to him. I don't think he saw though.

"So he's always been like this?" It comes out as more of a statement than a question, but Sebastian refutes it.

"Carter wasn't ever like this. He wasn't brutal, he was fair. He didn't..." Sebastian stops his thoughts again and this time a darker set of emotions plays on his face. "I should have never left," he confides in me and I give him a weak smile.

"If I could go back," he starts to say, but I cut him off, stating, "You can never go back."

The moment ends with silence as the car continues to move farther away. Closer and closer to the point in the road where I've chosen. The place where he turned around last time. Where he slowed down the most, and the farthest down the drive that he'll go.

"Why did you leave?" I ask Sebastian, more to distract him than anything else.

Sebastian doesn't even spare me a look as I reach for the lock. He's too busy pinching the bridge of his nose to keep whatever emotions are haunting him at bay.

Click. I shouldn't have turned to look at him, wasting the split second but also feeling guilty from the look of surprise and hurt on his face when he sees me rip the handle back and push the door outward.

He hears the lock click up though and his fingers wrap around my wrist, my left one with the deep gouges from the cuff last night. Fuck! The pain travels quickly and in a single electric motion. I hiss from the sudden jolt of pain as I rip my arm from his grasp, nearly falling out of the car until I have both feet on the ground and run as fast as I can. I don't stop.

Not for a moment. Not when he cusses and puts the car in park. Not when I nearly trip moving from asphalt to dirt as I enter the woods. Every breath hurts my lungs as I heave in air.

A few men's voices are carried into the woods. I know there are more men who guard the estate, but I don't know where they are. Somewhere they saw, which means they're close.

My legs are far too weak, and I can hear Sebastian's car door open and then his hard steps on the pavement as I whip past branches. More men shout and the tree limbs lash out at me as if to punish me, and I take it. I take every bite of the thin boughs and when I get to a sudden edge, I fling myself over, eager to get away. To fall hard, and that's exactly what I do. Landing on my back, I hit the cold dirt and roll.

My palm braces against something at the same time my legs bash into the rough trunk of a tree. The bark tears at my legs and I bite down to keep from screaming in agony. It hurts to stand up, but I do. Feeling lightheaded and weak, I stumble at first but keep moving. The voices sound farther away now. I hope they are.

I don't know which way is which, but I run as fast and hard as I can. I can't outrun Sebastian; he's far too big, and I've never been a runner. But I'll hear him when he comes, and I can at least hide.

"Fuck!" Sebastian's voice reverberates in the forest and it sends birds flying out of the treetops. Their sudden movement makes my heart lurch, and I'm staring up at them as I run into something hard.

Something with hands.

Something that grabs me.

The scream in my throat is held back by a large hand over my mouth.

My heart thumps and my anxiety spikes wildly until he shushes me, holding my small body close to his and hiding behind a thick tree.

"Shh, be calm, Ria." Nikolai's voice is the most comforting thing I could have asked for in this moment. Tiny cuts on my arms and face sting as I cling to Nikolai. Tears burn in the back of my eyes.

"I've got you now."

Chapter 16

Carter

"I thought there was nothing to talk about?" I answer the phone with Jase across from me. He's slow to take his seat in the chair but quiet as he does it. There's not a sound in the room other than my own heart beating until Marcus answers.

"I forgot I wanted to mention something," he tells me over the phone. "Are your brothers with you?" he asks me and then adds, "They may be interested to hear this as well."

"I've just messaged them," Jase answers and sets his phone down on the table. It vibrates with a response and then another.

"I'm glad you're here, Jase," Marcus says and I can hear the smile that must be plastered on his face. His voice carries through the space and over to the door as it opens, bringing

Daniel into the office. He's still catching his breath and slowing his pace after taking quick steps into the room.

"And which one is that?" Marcus asks as Declan comes in next, his tablet in hand. "Is it the one attempting to track me?" Marcus asks and instinctively I move my gaze to Declan. He merely stares at the phone on my desk, not answering.

"Of course we're trying to track you," I answer Marcus, slowly taking my seat and ignoring my own phone going off. "It's only fair, and you know it." He gives a low chuckle, but says nothing.

"What is it you want to tell us?" I ask him and glance at the monitor to see Sebastian's car parked in the street. I know he was talking to her. The nagging voice in my head is only concerned with Aria, but she's not even back yet. This call is going to be quick. First I'll handle this, and then I'll deal with Aria.

Soon. Soon I'll have her back, and I'll take Jase's advice.

"I have more information regarding the first time the lines were drawn in the sand," Marcus says. "Lines you failed to see."

"No more riddles." I cut Marcus off and grit my teeth before telling him, "I'm tired of games. Tell us who tried to take Addison and Aria." I harden my voice as I add, "I want names."

It's quiet for a second and then another, but Marcus eventually speaks.

"Jase, do you remember the articles I sent you?" Marcus asks and Jase's gaze narrows as he stares at the phone, not with anger, but with recollection. And we all look to him.

"About Tyler?" Jase asks and instantly my blood turns to ice. "The articles about the woman who hit him?" Jase clarifies and my mind races.

Lines drawn in the sand.

The first hit our family took.

"Tyler's death was an accident," Daniel speaks up and then visibly swallows, walking closer to the edge of the desk and daring the voice on the phone to deny that truth.

It was five years ago. Almost six now.

Tyler's death was before all this. Years ago. After I went against Talvery, once I started making a name for myself, yes. But I was no one. It's only in the last few years that my name has become synonymous with fear. Jase and I had barely gained ground, let alone anything worth the attention of hurting Tyler.

"His death was an accident," I say steadily, repeating Daniel's words.

Still, the coldness doesn't leave me. Slowly the memories come back of my youngest brother. He was the only good soul of the five of us. If ever a death was cruel, cutting his life short was just that.

"What were the articles?" I ask Jase, but Marcus answers instead.

"About her addictions..." Marcus's voice drawls until he says, "About her sudden death while waiting for her sentencing."

Daniel's face is pale and his eyes are glazed over. He saw it happen. He was there when Tyler was struck by her vehicle.

"What are you getting at?" I question Marcus, keeping my voice even and not letting the emotion get to me.

"She died in her sleep," Jase speaks over me and Marcus responds without hesitation, to say, "She was murdered."

"A name, Marcus," I remind him. "You wanted to tell us something, so tell us all of it. A woman being murdered in jail means nothing."

"No, but the name of the contract hit she was given, does. A hit I denied. The name was Jase Cross." Overwhelming nausea rises inside of me as Marcus weaves a tale and paints the picture of my past differently than I've ever seen it. "A small-town thug from Crescent Hills. A boy who was getting in the way and needed to be taken care of before he and his brothers gained too much ground. But she knew too much and had to die once she did her bidding."

"What?" Jase's voice carries disbelief as a growing numbness covers my skin with goosebumps.

"A hit?" Declan questions. Incredulity is written on his face.

I can't move. There's so much tension in every part of my body.

"Tony Romano came to me first." Hearing Romano's name sparks the need for vengeance, but I won't act quickly. I'll listen first, and assess. But imagining my youngest brother, only sixteen years old and dead in the street, proves that task to be futile. "He said either of the two would do, but settled on Jase." Marcus continues to tell his story while I wonder if it's possible. If it's true.

If Tyler was murdered all those years ago. If he took the place of Jase.

"The article I sent to Jase in particular was the biggest clue of all. His picture was there. What was he wearing, Jase?" Marcus leads Jase with the question, and it's only then that Jase's face crumples with torment. "Your hoodie." Marcus answers his own question, and I can hear Jase swallow.

"It was meant to be Jase, and she saw a boy who looked like him, on a rainy night in the same sweatshirt she was looking for. She wasn't a drunk driver, she was an alcoholic and drug addict hired by Romano because I refused."

"That's why you were there?" Daniel speaks up, his voice loud enough for Marcus to hear over the speaker. "You knew it was going to happen?"

"I thought it was going to be you. I wanted to save you. I had other plans for you." My throat's tight as I listen to Marcus, finding it harder and harder to disagree with his version of what happened. No matter how much I want to deny these revelations coming to light, years later.

"He wanted to end you, but instead he delivered a death that fueled both of you to conquer without remorse."

"Romano?" Declan questions, and we share a knowing look.

"Romano," Marcus confirms.

He's dead. He's fucking dead.

"Why now?" Daniel asks, not hiding the emotion in his voice. "You were there. You knew all this time and you didn't tell me back then, you didn't warn me… but now?"

"Why tell us this now?" Declan repeats Daniel's question.

"For one, you asked who tried to take Addison and Aria. I'm giving you an answer. But the other reason, the much bigger reason, is because I knew Carter would listen. I knew I'd have his attention." Marcus's voice lacks the same depth it had during his tale. Like he's snapped back to the present and he's no longer interested.

"You would've had my attention whenever you wanted it, Marcus," I tell him honestly.

"Yes," he answers, "but I didn't want it back then. I wanted it now." And with that, the line goes dead.

None of my brothers speak after the click fills the room.

He didn't want it back then?

Another riddle. I let the words sink in, but they hardly mean anything. Marcus has never lied. Romano had my brother killed. Romano has taken his last free breath.

"He's a dead man," I speak out loud although none of my brothers react.

Jase hasn't moved. He's as still as he can be, and Declan keeps looking between him and Daniel.

"It wasn't your fault," Daniel offers Jase, but Jase only

shakes his head.

Mourning the loss of a loved one is the worst feeling in the world. There's no drug that can take that pain away, because there's no drug that can bring them back. They're simply gone forever.

But to learn the truth of a tragedy, to learn that there was more to the story, more than what you were told before and to still have no control, it adds salt to the wound.

And for Jase... he's in fucking agony, knowing it was supposed to be him.

The vibrations from my phone are a muted distraction. I don't even know how long it's been going off – Jase's is going off too - and I'm eager to pick it up, only to realize what Marcus meant.

He didn't want my attention back then. He wanted it now, because he didn't want my attention elsewhere.

Anger ignites inside me like never before as I read the message out loud. "Aria's gone."

I'll kill them all.

Chapter 17

Aria

My heart won't stop racing. It's all moving so fast. One decision could change the course of everything. I didn't know when I walked through that gate that it would happen like this, moving easily from one side to the other. I was foolish to think I could just run away from this life. The thought echoes in the chambers of my mind as my left foot crunches the twigs on the ground and my right side leans heavier into Nikolai. He's walking so fast, pulling me in closer to him. It's all moving too fast.

There are small scratches everywhere. My jeans are torn and covered in dirt and my arms are smeared with blood. What's worse is that I can't stop shaking. I think it's just the adrenaline, or maybe it's due to anxiety. I don't know which, but I can't stop shaking and it makes Nikolai hold me that much tighter.

The branches crack beneath our feet with every step and I keep looking back. They must hear us. It's darker with every passing moment, and I don't know where we're going but it doesn't matter; Nikolai leads me away. *Nikolai will be the one Carter blames.*

Every small sound behind us makes me jump, but even then, I'm not given a moment to stop; Nikolai doesn't let up. I can hear his heart pounding, and I know he knows he's dead if Carter's men catch us before we get out of here.

I don't think he'd hurt me, but he'll kill Nikolai.

"He can't find us together." The words rush from me as I reach up and grab Nikolai's shirt, forcing him to stop and think. "He can't think you took me; he'll kill you. He can't--" the words don't stop tumbling out of me, but Nik hushes me.

"I have you, and I don't care if he knows it." He's surprisingly calm, and justified in his response. "I've waited too long to get close enough to save you." My thoughts race, wondering how he even got through Carter's security, where they are and how long Nikolai has waited out here for this moment.

"How did you know?" I ask him, my eyes searching his for all of the answers.

"Someone told me to come. He told me I'd be able to save you." As he speaks, Nik's voice is full of so many emotions. "I'm sorry it took so long, Ria," he says, his voice cracking as he grips my waist and urges me forward. I stumble, refusing to move and waiting for him to look back at me. I need him to realize how serious this is.

"He's going to kill you," I say and stare deep into his light blue eyes, knowing it's true. Before I can urge him to run, he tells me, "Not if I kill him first."

"Don't talk like that." The words are torn from my throat, immediate and raw, just as instincts are. Betrayal flashes in Nikolai's eyes and I wish I could take the words back, if only to ease his pain, but I can't. He's stunned and pained, crushed from my words, but it doesn't last long.

The sound of heavy footsteps behind us forces me to crush myself into Nik's embrace. Gripping onto his shirt, I beg him in a whisper, "Run."

I can feel his large hand splayed along my shoulder, pulling me closer to him as he whispers against my hair, "Never. Never again."

My face is buried in his chest when I hear my name called out behind me. For a moment I imagine any way that I can barter my life for Nikolai's, but I don't believe for one second that Carter would negotiate with me. Not when I have no control and nothing left to offer.

The moment is short lived, because I hear the voice again. So familiar, yet it feels as if it's been forever since I last heard my cousin Brett.

Shock forces me to pull away from Nik, but again

everything happens so fast. Even as he grabs me in a bear hug, Brett drags me along the edge of the woods to a dirt road where an old, beat-up truck is idling. There are two other men with us, but I don't remember their names and with Brett clinging to my side, I don't have time to ask.

"I'm so sorry, Ria," my cousin keeps saying as we move to the truck. "I'm a bastard and a coward, and I'm sorry."

"It's okay," I tell him repeatedly, not knowing what else to say or how to comfort him. Or where the fuck he came from. "I told you to run," is all I can settle on, but he shakes his head, remorse flooding his eyes.

"Two in the back, armed and ready." Nik gives the command as the truck door swings open with a creak that carries through the woods.

"Ria." Brett says my name reverently before hugging me one last time and helping me up into the truck. The dried leather seats are cracked. I've never seen this car in my entire life.

"Don't worry, it's sound, just made to look like it's something to be ignored," Nik says, as if reading my mind. My gaze finds his as the truck sways with Brett and one of the other guys climbing into the back and under a tarp, guns slipped through inconspicuous holes. This truck was made for getaways. The quiet hum of the engine is all I hear for a moment.

It's only then that I feel like it's real. Like I'm actually leaving Carter and going home.

Going back to my father and his men.

The two other men I can't place, although their faces are so familiar, but their names still elude me in this moment. I can feel their eyes on me as they climb into the back, assessing, judging, and questioning. Wanting to know what happened and more importantly, whose side I'm on, I'm sure.

He let me get away. It's all I can think. Carter let them take me. That's the only way it could be this easy.

The thought brings a swell of emotion up my throat and I feel like I'm going to be sick again. The dry heave forces me to open the door and lean out of it. The air is cold against the sudden heat spreading through my body and traveling up to my face.

Everything is quiet as the sickness leaves me. It's disgusting and leaves an acidic burn in its wake. But even when it's over, I can't bring myself back into the car fully. I lean out of it, feeling the cool air and wishing I could leave as easily as the wind can.

It's all too much. It's all too fast and I hold my belly, not knowing what to think or what to do.

It's only when Nik gently rubs my back and whispers that we have to leave that I resign myself to the fate I chose.

"I didn't plan for this," I confess to Nikolai as he pulls me back into the truck and gives me a napkin to wipe my mouth.

I didn't plan to leave the man I love. I didn't plan on him allowing it.

I didn't plan to run back to my family, to his enemy.

And I didn't plan for the small life I wanted to protect from all of this.

I needed to run to get away. Not to fall back into the same game, only to find the color of my pieces have changed.

"He's going to hate me," I cry out softly and once again, Nikolai pulls me into him. The truck is still idle and I know time is ticking. Precious time.

Nik calls out for one of the guys to come drive and scoots to the middle so he can comfort me, even as I cry over Carter.

As the other man gets into the driver's seat, giving me a look of sympathy, Nik reaches behind the seat and pulls out a thick, wool blanket.

"It's all right," Nik tells me, not taking the moment to curse Carter or question my sanity. "We're going home."

For the first ten minutes, I kept expecting bullets to fly out of nowhere. I was ready for the ping of steel to slam against the truck. And then I thought maybe Carter would just appear in front of the truck. Standing in the middle of the road like a madman.

It took too long for me to swallow the jagged pill. I've truly left Carter. He's not coming to take me back.

"You don't have to tell me now." Nik's voice slices through my thoughts. The man at the wheel, a man named Connor, glances at me. I know he's curious. I can't imagine what everyone thinks of me, knowing I chose to stay with Carter when they came to rescue me.

Shamefully, I consider making up a lie, just so they won't know how I've fallen for him and how I betrayed them by doing so. The idea comes and goes with the rumble of the truck being carried into the fall air.

"You don't have to tell me right now," he repeats and I gaze into Nik's eyes as he continues, "but I need to know everything you remember." He nods slightly, as if wanting me to agree to such a thing.

"You don't want to know, Nik," I answer him, feeling the painful fissure again in my chest. My cheeks heat as I stare down at my hands and pull away from him. I start to tell him that I love Carter and that I only ran because he doesn't love me in a way that's healthy. I only ran because I can't bear to think of a child growing up in this world we inhabit. I wanted to run away from it all, but as the truck jostles over a bump, I know I only ran into another hell.

"You're safe now," Connor says calmly from his seat. It takes me a long second to remember who he is. To place his face and his voice. Turning around in my seat, I remember the other man from when we were younger. The memories pooling together and reminding me who I am.

"How about I tell you a secret?" Nik offers. He sets his hand on my thigh and rubs a soothing circle with the pad of his thumb. He's so much taller than me, I have to crane my neck to look up at him after watching him swallow.

The air changes instantly, tensing and becoming thick. Too thick as Nik starts, "Do you remember the day we met? At my father's funeral when we were just kids?"

My pulse feels weak as I answer him, knowing deep inside of me that Nikolai will never hurt me, but also feeling that whatever he's about to tell me, whatever it is, is going to cause me pain. It's the look in his eyes. I recognize it too well.

"You have to wait for me to finish," Nik presages his confession, and I nod. "Tell me you will. Promise me, Ria," he commands me, his voice hardening.

I glance at Connor, who cautiously looks back to us before I tell Nikolai, "I promise." With a quick breath I add, "I'll let you finish."

Butterflies flutter in the pit of my stomach as Nikolai says, "I was working for Romano at the funeral. When my father died, I was working for Romano."

The words hit me over and over. *Working for Romano*. A revolting wave of nausea spreads through me as Nikolai swallows and peers down at me, waiting for a response. I can't breathe.

Romano. The man who took me and traded me for a war. The man who would have seen me dead that night I killed Stephan rather than to have his ally murdered.

My body stiffens and I can't control it. I've never feared

Nikolai, not until this moment.

"Romano told me your father had my father killed. That's why I was so angry when you touched me. When you came over to me as if you had any right to."

I can't swallow and I struggle to breathe.

"I don't know what my father--" I battle the need to explain, to defend, to do whatever I have to do to survive with the anger that slowly rises. Lies. My life has been built on so many lies and with so many men I can't trust.

Nikolai cuts me off. "It doesn't matter. None of it matters, Ria."

I have to bite down on my lip to keep from screaming at him not to call me by the name my mother called me. The betrayal and rage stir inside of me, brewing a cocktail I'm not sure I can control.

My best friend. My only friend. Deceived me for years. He was a rat. A fucking rat!

"Your father told me that it was Romano who'd done it. That Romano had my father killed. And I didn't know who to believe. I had no one, yet both of them had hired me. I was only a kid; I was angry and more than that, I was scared and so fucking lonely."

The truck moves steadily along until we're out of the brush and dirt road entirely, headed down a back road of thin asphalt.

The day at the funeral comes back to me slowly with the quiet rumble, the picture painted in a different hue than I've seen it before.

"I'm still the same, Ria. You have to understand. I was a kid, and you don't say no to men like your father... or to men like Romano."

"Did my father know?" I manage to ask him as the anger wanes and the boy in my memory looks back at me. I remember his face. I remember the anger and I remember how he held me in return. How I needed someone just like he did. He was my someone. But the lies... I'm so sick of the sins and secrets.

"No." His answer is solemn. "Romano wanted me to keep eyes on Talvery, and Talvery hired me to do shit work. I figured one day, one of them would kill me." Nik's voice is resigned and flat, with no motive revealed in his words other than survival. "Romano would kill me for not telling him everything. Or your father, for being a rat. I didn't want this. I was only a boy."

Through my lashes, I peek at Connor, who doesn't respond. That's when it hits me that Connor knew too.

Adrenaline spikes through me, numbing me as Connor's gaze catches mine.

"I don't work for Romano," Connor tells me before I have to ask. "But I've known what Nik has – all of us have – for years."

My gut churns. My throat's tight as I look up at Nik. "You didn't tell me?" The words are merely whispers.

Nik doesn't speak, he only looks down at me with regret, but Connor answers in his place. "Your father will kill us if he finds out we know, Aria." I can barely tear my gaze from Nik to look back at Connor. "You didn't deserve to be put in the middle."

The irony of his words aren't lost on me.

"I had to stay and as everything happened, I did what I had to do to survive."

"You didn't have to stay," I argue.

"Yes, I did."

"Why did you stay? You could have left any time and just run." I push the words out, containing my anger that's dimming, and remembering all the times we've been together. At one time in my life, he was my everything, and yet, he held onto secrets that could have destroyed me.

It's quiet for so long, I start to think I didn't ask the question, until I look up at him.

He stares back at me with such pain in the depths of his haunted eyes. Pain that I don't already know, yet somewhere deep in my soul I did know. I've always known.

"I could never leave you, Ria," he tells me and then rips his gaze away to look straight ahead as his eyes gloss over.

"Then why let them take me?" I ask him and swallow the hard lump growing in my throat. "You gave me to Romano!" My voice raises and I can't help it, but as it does, Nik grips me tighter and peers at me with a fierceness that's undeniable.

He told me that he's the reason I was taken. It's Nikolai's fault all of this started. If he loved me so much, why would he dare risk it?

"No, I didn't. He fucked me over, and he'll pay for that." Nik's jaw is hard and his eyes dark with anger. The kind of anger that I've seen before. Anger that comes with revenge.

"I wanted you away from this life," he confesses to me, his shoulders relaxing as he stares out the window behind me. "Your father is getting older. Everyone knows his time is coming to an end. What do you think would have happened to you?"

I don't answer Nik's question.

"He promised he'd save you. I lured you out, taking your notebook, and I knew you'd try to retrieve it. I knew you'd think it was Mika. And Romano lied to me. I'm sorry, Ria. Your father doesn't have long, and I needed to protect you. I needed you away from all of this."

"It wasn't your decision to make," is all I can say to him. My notebook. It's an odd feeling to have an object mean so much in a life where nothing is meaningful anymore.

"I can't believe it was all you."

"I had to save you," he tells me and settles back into his seat, apparently done with the conversation.

It's hard not to blame it all on him. Everything I've gone through. I struggle with all the emotions running through my blood.

"You love him, don't you?" he asks me with a hint of disgust in his tone. "He's brainwashed you." He gives himself an explanation without waiting for my response.

"I do," I say, staring Nikolai right in the eye. "I love Carter Cross..." I have to swallow before finishing. "But I'm not dumb enough to think we'd last... Because he doesn't love me. Not how I need."

My heart does this awful thing just then. It pumps, but it's lifeless. It beats, but there's no sound. It gives up on me in this moment, and I can feel it as it happens.

It's a lie on my lips. I hear a whisper in the back of my head.

I have to remember why I left. I have to remember this life and what it does to people.

"I need to get out of here," I murmur beneath my breath, not to Nikolai or Connor, but to myself.

"I can help you," Nik is quick to tell me, pulling me close to him although I'm still in his grasp. "I'll make it right. I'll get you out of here, Ria. I just have to do one thing first."

Chapter 18

Carter

"Of course he'd bring her back to him." The words are accompanied by silence as we watch Nikolai and his crew pull up and wait for the gates of the Talvery estate to open.

She didn't run to Nikolai – or even to her father. I fucking know she didn't. She ran, and she had good reason with the way I treated her, but she didn't run to him.

I saw the footage.

"I'm sorry," Sebastian says from the back of the Grand Cherokee SRT. The black SUV sits in the shadows. With tinted windows and an engine that can hit sixty miles per hour in four point eight seconds, it's our go-to vehicle, armed and equipped for anything coming our way.

We got it years ago so we could haul ass after making hits.

As we sit idle along the forest two miles away from the Talvery estate, I don't give a fuck about speeding away from anything. Not without Aria.

"She was going to run however she could," I mutter under my breath at the driver's seat, excusing Sebastian.

"Still…" he mumbles, running his hand through his hair. He can barely look at me and I hate it. It's not his fault she ran. It's not his fault she got away. It's mine.

The wheel is hot under my grip and everything inside of me is pushing me to get out and storm the front doors of her father's estate.

Which would leave me dead on the polished marble front steps.

She's so fucking close, but out of my reach as the neatly trimmed bushes that line the path to the door sway with the wind on the screen. I've only been closer to this property once in my life.

At the mercy of her father when I was just a boy.

I swallow down the memory as the car door opens and several men with machine guns approach Nik's beat-up truck.

That fucking prick.

My heart slams in my chest when I see her. Her brunette locks tumble around her shoulders. Her shirt's torn and there's still dirt covering half of her ass all the way down her leg.

She doesn't carry herself like the girl she used to be. Her head is held high and her shoulders are straight, but the fear is still there, dancing in her doe eyes.

As much as she can't hide that she's a woman meant for this life, she can't hide the fear it brings her to be caught in the middle of a war either.

Aria doesn't stop looking all around her as Nikolai ushers her into the front door, looking over his shoulder in the direction of the camera we've hacked into. As if he knows we're here.

It's only when the men surround her, that I realize how quiet it is in the SUV.

The shame and regret hardly register anymore. Shame from the way I've treated her. And regret for it all.

"I'll do better by her," I tell them and still not a damn man speaks up. I see Sebastian nod in my periphery and I have to close my eyes and take in a steadying breath before opening them to see Nikolai's hand on the small of Aria's back. And then the large front door closes.

"It'll be different when the war is over," Jase offers and Sebastian agrees. As if any of it is because of the war.

"It'll be less complicated." Daniel chimes in.

"Less need to fight," Declan adds.

It was never the war though. It's my fault.

Knowing Nik's with her eases some of the strain coursing through me. The jealousy is present as always, but I don't have time for that. He'll protect her, and that's the only saving grace I have right now. Nikolai won't let a damn thing happen to her, and I owe him for that. I know more about Nikolai than any other Talvery man for one reason. He's the one who was always with Aria. He's the one I wanted every detail on. And he does love her, I know he does. I owe him more than I'll ever let him know.

He can be her hero for the moment. He can protect her.

I don't give a fuck if I'm nothing but the villain who captures her.

The villain who holds her against her will until her will changes.

The villain who will put an end to this war and to the empire her last name gives power to.

The villain who will stop at nothing to have her completely.

And the rest of me, whatever is left, the rest of me will belong to her. Always.

I don't have a choice; that is all I'll accept.

And she'll learn to accept it too.

"We already know the place, and we have the count on the men." Jase is the first to get to business. Tonight, Talvery will finally fall.

There are eight men at the front entrance. Another four towers along the tall brick walls that surround the property. Each of them with a handful of men armed and ready.

There will be even more men inside. They'll have to die as well.

"Wherever we hit will be a distraction," Declan says as if

he's thinking out loud, "but they'll also send Talvery into the safe room."

"We need to contain him and Aria too if we can," Jase responds to Declan's statement, leaning forward in his seat to stare at the blueprints on the tablet.

"The safe room is large, but if we get rid of it as an option, they'll have nowhere to go, they're outnumbered... it's just the matter of the safe room and if there's anything at all that we don't see."

"Hit the safe room first then," I answer without thinking twice, but then add, turning to face Jase, "Unless they take Aria there."

Her locked away in a room, refusing to let me in even though she knows I'll be waiting for her and only time is keeping her away from me, is exactly what our relationship has been. I can see it reversed though just as easily.

Tonight I take that option away. Tonight I change the course of our fate. I choose us. Forever. No more fighting; I've fought enough in this life already. I only want to love her.

"Is everyone in place?" I ask Jase and he nods solemnly. We left our home and every piece of property we own unguarded. Every single man is here. Every man ready for blood. The only exception is a small crew guarding Addison right now, far away from all of this.

"I've got the security feeds." As Declan speaks, my eyes open and I wait for the screen to flick to a new video stream, one that shows the hacked footage inside each and every one of Talvery's rooms until it lands on a picture of Aria.

The images flick by on the screen, moving as she moves, and focused on her expression.

My poor Aria. Fuck, I've never known pain like this before.

"You're good for something, Declan," Daniel tells him, with his hand on the loaded gun in his lap.

"Fuck you too," Declan replies with a smirk.

"Feels like old times," Jase says and I turn to look at him, looking at each of my brothers and Sebastian. It does.

"It's been a while, hasn't it?" I tell him, feeling each pulse in my veins. The tension, the buildup. But something else too.

"Since it's felt like everything is riding on this one moment?"

"Yeah," I answer him.

"Too long," Sebastian says lowly, checking his gun and then slamming the magazine into place with the butt of his hand.

"It used to be thrilling, though," Jase says quietly, glancing at the screen showing the men outside the door to where Aria's been taken. A few men wait outside, but Nikolai goes in with her. "This is different."

"There's too much riding on this one," I tell them all and their nods are instant.

"We'll get her and bring her home," Jase tells me and Sebastian looks between the two of us.

"When this is over," Sebastian says, "I'm not leaving. I'll

bring Chloe home; she'll come with me." I don't have time to answer him.

"First Talvery, then Romano. Your ass isn't going anywhere." Jase's answer pulls Sebastian's lips into an asymmetric smirk.

It's hard to let the words go, but I tell my brothers something I often don't. "Thank you." I swallow thickly and then turn to each of them, the leather seats groaning as I do. "Thank you for being here. For helping me and for helping her."

"Of course," Jase says, his eyes searching mine and the sad smile showing. "We survived together. Fought together... Loved together."

"I wouldn't be anywhere else. You need me," Sebastian tells me and looks me in the eyes. "Mostly because I fucked up, but still, you need me."

His joke lightens the mood a touch, enough to let the other emotions in just slightly. The emotions that remind me she left me. The ones that prove to me it's because of me.

With his hand gripping my shoulder, Sebastian tells me, "We'll get her back."

"And I'll keep her," I tell them, meaning every word. I'll keep all of her every way I know how.

"All right, enough with this shit," Declan says, and Daniel huffs a short laugh. It's been a long time since I've had a conversation like this one. One that's real, and touches a piece of me that remains dormant. A piece Aria holds hostage.

"I've got it all covered now," Declan speaks up from the back of the SUV. "The safe room is empty, but it's not close enough to the outside rooms to be hit easily."

"Does Aden have vision anywhere near the safe room?"

"He can hit the west side through the hall window, send in the smoke bombs and ambush that side of the house. We'll be in and out with the bombs within a few minutes, but they'll react. The odds of coming out are not the best." Jase answers for Declan, and I can see the plan already formulating in his head.

Aden is already waiting on the other side. They're waiting for Jase's cue.

"We need to hit them all at once," I tell Jase. The adrenaline in my blood is nearly suffocating me. Only because I'm sitting here. I need to move, to get this shit over with and have her back. "Tell them all to hit on my command."

As I say the words, the vision on the screen changes and it turns back to Aria. Her arms are crossed tight, and she stands by herself awkwardly in the center room. Facing Nikolai, neither of them moving, but both of them the picture of regret.

There's no fucking way I won't do everything I can to hold on to her.

"Hit the towers, the front entrance, and the safe room all at once. We have more men than they do." The words leave me the second the screen changes again.

"What about Romano?" Declan asks.

"What about him?" The anger and hate in Daniel's tone

reflects the same in every single one of us.

"He could try to make a move on us while our backs are turned," Declan says and then cuts to a feed showing his men lining the territory. They're ready to strike, waiting for Talvery to weaken. If we bring them down first, Romano will have us surrounded and if he desired, he could strike.

"He doesn't know we know, not yet," Jase answers him and then Sebastian states, "We'll keep the north side the strongest for Talvery, pushing his men toward the heaviest side Romano has armed. We don't have to kill them all, just enough to outnumber them. Enough to make them realize Talvery, the name, the empire, is no more."

"It's just like before, no one willingly dies for a dead man." Jase's eyes shine with the memories of all the challengers we've taken down in the past. The name Talvery may be old, it may hold power, but when the man is dead, the name will mean nothing.

"What's the plan?" Jase asks me and then adds, "Step by step."

"We need to get in close first," I tell him. "She's in the east wing, so we can cut the feeds, take out the east tower discreetly with no bombs, make our approach through that way and once we're in, hit the other towers and the safe room."

"They'll be looking everywhere but at us," Jase responds, nodding his head and breathing in deep. "You go in and get her, Bastian and I will come with and take out whoever comes running."

"Kill the feeds as soon as we get close to the east tower. We'll walk along the tree line," I tell Declan and he's quick to answer, "The cameras rotate every ninety seconds. You're going to need the feeds handled before you get past this road. Or else they'll see you coming."

"There are men on the ground," Jase pipes up. "Cut the feeds, we'll get in there, kill those two fuckers outside the east tower and use them to get in."

Sebastian looks at Declan and asks, "It's fingerprints right?" With a nod from Declan, Jase adds, "Dead fuckers still have prints. It'll work."

With my brother and my friend behind me, my men surrounding the enemy and ready to wage war, it's time. My heart pounds as I run through the forest and raise my gun, hearing the startled shouts from the towers regarding the security feeds going down. I can hear their fear; I can fucking feel it as I raise my gun in the shadows. The three of us shoot, the bullets muffled with the silencers, before the two men, men just like me, even see us. The first two men to die tonight. Their bodies are still warm, heavy and limp as we drag them to the security pad, wipe the blood from their fingers on our pants to gain entrance, and begin to end this war.

Chapter 19

Aria

"I can't see you with him." Nikolai's voice is calm, somehow sounding forgiving as he watches me pace in my father's office.

I stare past him at the pictures on my father's wall. There's a picture of my mother and father, with my uncle between them. I never met him. In the photo he's holding them close, his arms wrapped around their shoulders. It's a black-and-white snapshot, taken just before my uncle was murdered. It's only one of nearly a dozen pictures on the wall to the right of my father's desk. But only that photo, and one other hold any of my attention.

I breathe in and out slowly as I stare at the second picture, trying to stand upright and not let on that anything's wrong.

It's Carter's house. The Cross brothers' home. The same photograph that's in Carter's foyer. An icy prick spreads over my skin and all I can hear are my shallow breaths.

I swear it's the same. I knew when I first saw it that the picture was familiar. I thought maybe I'd been there before, but this is why it was so familiar.

My father has a picture of Carter's old house, the house he destroyed, hung up in his office. Is it a fucking trophy? A reminder of something? My stomach roils as I cross my arms tighter, feeling more and more like a trapped animal. I wish my father were here so I could ask him. So I could face him after everything that's happened. If he were though... I can't even imagine where we'd begin. A lifetime has come and gone. I'm not the same person I was when I last stepped foot in this home.

It doesn't matter though. He's not here, and I doubt he'll come for me until he has the time. Business has always come first.

"What did he do to you, Ria?" Nik asks me and I turn to him. Seated in the whiskey-colored leather wingback chair in the corner of the room, I see Nikolai in a different light than I ever have before.

Not as my friend or former lover, not as the boy who needed me. But as a man in pain and on edge, reckless and wanting change, needing it and ready to take it.

I see him as a danger.

"Nikolai, you're scaring me," I whisper with a quietness that begs for them to stay silent, but somehow the words find him. The corner of his lips drag down as his eyes flick with a light of recognition.

"I don't mean to, I just don't think you realize what has to happen," he tells me and then swallows with a look of anguish in his features.

"What has to happen?" I ask him, feeling my hands go cold as I stand aimlessly in the room. Knowing I'm once again at the mercy of men who find me lacking.

"Today men will die."

"Men die every day," I'm quick to respond and he gives me a sad smirk with his huff, leaning forward with his elbows on his knees. He stares at the floor and not at me. His eyes close as I whip around to the door of the office, hearing shouts echo down the halls. The feeds are down. Nik's cell phone goes off, but only for a second before he silences it and his gaze moves from it to me.

"It's all right. You had to know he'd come for you," he tells me, his eyes begging me to deny it, but he already knows the truth.

The pounding in my chest intensifies, and a warmth spreads through me but not nearly enough to stop frigidness that clings to me.

"Will you hate me if I made it easier?" Nik asks me, shifting his weight and reaching behind him for the gun tucked in the back of his pants. "If I killed him, would you hate me?" he asks me but shakes his head before I can even answer. My lips are parted and the words are there, *yes, I'll hate you forever if you kill him*. The pleas not to are the same I've heard before, spoken from my own mouth.

"You know that I love you," he tells me and then he adds, "And you know he's no good for you." I watch the muscles in his neck tense as he swallows. He stands and pulls a drawer open in my father's desk, taking another gun, checking that it's loaded and placing it on the desk before closing the door.

"You ran from him... But still, you want him to live."

"I can't explain it," I tell Nikolai, watching every small movement.

He peeks up at me, hearing the trace of fear in my words and lowers his head. "I'd never hurt you, Ria. Stop looking at me like I would."

"There are different kinds of pain. And I've recently come to accept that some people, some men very close to me, can't help but to cause me the worst kinds of pain."

"Don't compare me to him," he retorts, and the menace in his voice is as chilling as the sharpness in his eyes when he looks at me.

The sarcastic and flat response comes from a place of pain deep inside of me. "How dare I do such a thing."

"You're just sick." Nikolai speaks more to himself than to me. "You'll see. When this is all over, you'll see."

"I've thought long and hard about that. About whether or not I was sick," I tell him as he rounds the desk and leans against the front of it. "I think maybe for a moment I was. Maybe when I wasn't well, and I know I wasn't well because of him. But I can see clearly now. And I'm thinking more about myself these days." My fingers itch to touch my lower belly, but I don't. I don't want him to know or anyone else. I'll bide my time and then I'll run far, far away. I'll be someone else. And leave all traces of Aria Talvery and this world behind.

"Don't you think if you were sick, you wouldn't know it?"

I nod once, feeling a strength rise inside of me. "You're not wrong, but the thing is, even if I am sick, I like who I am more now than I did before. I see the world for what it is, and I'm stronger for it." I don't tell Nikolai, but deep inside I know I can be whoever I choose. I can do whatever I choose to do.

At this moment, running is what I choose, because I want this child to live a life surrounded by love. And I don't know if it's possible to have that with Carter. No matter how much I love him or how much he thinks he loves me. He doesn't know how to love. And I won't allow that life for my child.

At that thought, it feels as if a jagged nail runs down the length of my chest from the inside. Tearing at me. It's not right and it's not fair, but nothing about this tale has been.

"You're strong, Aria, but I can give you a world where you don't have to be," Nikolai tells me. His voice caresses the pain that cascades over me. Three scenarios play in my mind, warring within.

One where Nikolai holds me like he used to. Where I look at him with the love and desire that used to be, and then I look down to a small child in my arms, one who doesn't belong to him. A baby who will forever remind me that I don't love Nikolai nearly as much as I once loved another. Nikolai would take care of me, he'd love me and provide for not just me, but also this baby. And I would use him; I know deep in my heart that's all it would ever be.

Another version of the fucked-up fairytale has me back on Carter's bed, cross-legged with an infant nestled and bundled in my lap while I peek up at the man I love, sitting across the room in a chair, watching me from a distance he chooses.

The father of my child.

The beast of a man.

If things were different, I'd never leave his side. But wishes and hopes do nothing. Things aren't different, and I won't raise a child with the venom and tension that comes with standing by Carter's side.

And in the third vision, the one I choose, I'm alone on a quiet porch, rocking an infant in my arms. I see the small home set back in the distance off a dirt road. Away from it all. Maybe a boy or maybe a girl, but either way, there will be no hate, no vengeance that lingers around us. The wind will whisper lullabies and although this baby won't have a father, I'll give him or her everything I have and protect them from what I once was and this vicious world I came from.

One day I'll tell him a story so raw and so true that he won't believe it. It will only be a fairytale gone wrong. More importantly, that child will be stronger and better than I ever will be. I can't choose a better life for myself. But I can give one to this little life.

"I love you, Nikolai," I whisper as I open my eyes and then I make sure he sees me, really sees me before I tell him, "but it's not the love you have for me. And I love another more than you."

"You left him," Nikolai reminds me and I nod my head, feeling the rawness scratch up my throat.

"If he would have shown me the love I needed, I would still be with him." I let my hand travel to my stomach, where I know Nikolai sees as I tell him, "Right now I can't risk anything."

The door to the office swings open without notice, bringing with it the sound of my father's voice. "Still be with who?" The words sound cautious. My heart races as he slowly closes the door behind him and the lights go out, darkness taking over until the backup power comes on.

My father stares behind me, sharing a look with Nikolai before looking back at me. My breaths come in quick pants.

"Father," I breathe out, and I don't know what to think. I don't know what to do. In many ways I feel like his enemy. Simply because I've fallen into bed, but also in love with the man who longs to see my father take his last breath.

"Still be with Carter?" my father questions, walking closer to me, each step feeling intimidating.

I can only swallow until he lets out a deep breath and looks down at me with sympathy. "I didn't hear everything," he says, his eyes flicking to Nikolai before finding my gaze again and continuing, "but child, this isn't your fault, and I'm sorry." A sudden wave of relief flows through me. My lungs are still and refuse to move, even with the reassurance. "It's all right, Aria." My father's voice is calm and gives nothing but comfort. I can't help but to move to him and as I do, he opens his arms.

To be loved unconditionally is something so rare. But from a parent to a child, there is forgiveness in every moment. The guarded walls crumble even though I'm so aware of Nikolai behind me and my father in front of me, coming forward to pull me in close. He whispers it isn't my fault. His words are apologetic.

He holds me close to him, he holds me like he has before, but back when I was a child. Back when I let him.

"I'm so sorry, Aria," he says and holds me tight, although his voice is tense.

"It's not your fault," I tell him, because it's true. This is the life we lead and breed. No one is to blame for the hate and havoc it brings. It simply exists.

"I'm scared," I confess against his chest. The smell of soft leather and spiced cologne wraps around me just as his arms do.

"You think you love him, and considering what he did, I understand." It's almost shocking to hear his words, but then he whispers, "I'm not sorry that I have to kill him."

My body stiffens in his embrace but if my father realizes that, he doesn't let on. A single breath leaves me and my eyes open, staring at the wall across from my father's desk where the pictures stare back at me. "I should have done it long ago," he says as I pull back slightly, wanting nothing more than to run once again. *Run far, far away*, I think as my fingers drift past my belly and I back away from my father. Pulling back from my father, I see his eyes are as cold and dark as they ever were.

One step, then two.

The second step comes with the shaking of the ground. A rumble at first, but then a movement so sharp, I nearly lose my step.

Bombs. One after another and seemingly all around us. Harsh intakes of air. A spike of fear and adrenaline.

We're under attack. And I don't know if it's Romano.... or if it's Carter coming for me.

Men scream, but not the two I'm with though. They're silent as I fall to the ground on my ass and move to the edge of the room. To hide in the corner and brace myself there. The explosions are close, but not close enough to hit us. Still, they keep coming. Each one sounding closer than the last.

Nikolai and my father don't seek cover like I do. They act like they expected it as they simply brace against the wall of the room, letting each rocking blow hit without a difference in their expression.

The ground shakes and the sounds of explosions reverberate through the room. The bombs must be close, because the shelves jostle and with it, books fall. I watch the gun as it rattles on the desk, the metal skimming along the edge as it finds its way closer to falling, but somehow manages to hang on, even as the monitor crashes to the floor, cracking the frame and forcing a scream from me with the next loud explosion.

That makes seven.

The lamp's shifted to the edge of the desk, where it topples in slow motion at the last blast. It hits the gun Nikolai left there on the corner, and my father's gaze lingers on the steel.

"Boss." Nik's voice is stern, direct, almost a statement rather than a question and the hard gaze between two men verifies my father recognizes that too.

"What can I do to help?" Nik's question is casual, at ease this time.

"Seven," I whisper the word, daring to go against the wishes of my frozen body. The only thing I can feel is the numbing tingle of fear. But I counted seven. "Seven explosions." My father's eyes stay on mine and only when he turns his attention to Nikolai am I able to breathe again.

He doesn't answer me, he doesn't say a damn word to me as I stay where I am, hunkered down and counting each second from now until another bomb will hit. But the next one never comes.

The heavy footsteps carry through the room and in time with my quickened pulse as my father walks around his desk, kicking his fallen computer as he does. My shoulders hunch forward and my eyes slam shut at the cracking sound of the screen.

I shudder again when Nikolai lays a hand on my back, splayed and meant to comfort. I can't help but to let out a short cry and back away until I see it's him.

"Fuck," I gasp out and try to calm my racing heart. It's too much. This world is too much.

"You're all right here," Nik tells me and the moment he does, my father commands him away.

"Get down to the west wing. Get Connor and the rest of them. Block anyone who comes in." I've never seen my father look the way he does now. With both of his hands lightly placed on his desk as he stands at its head, everything on top of the sleek black surface is in disarray and even the paintings behind him are crooked.

The room reflects nothing of the controlled, powerful man who's ruled from that very spot for years. And neither does the look in his eyes. There's a sadness wrapped around the dark swirls of his gaze. And a sense of acceptance, plus a tiredness I've never seen.

"Dad?" I dare to speak up, and he dares to ignore me.

"Block off the hall and kill anyone who enters." He doesn't speak to me. Only to Nikolai.

A crease lines the center of Nik's forehead as he gestures to the phone in his hand, the screen of it brightening with notifications every few seconds. "There's no sign of anyone-"

"I know! You don't think I saw the messages?" my father screams at him with hurried words. Anger and fear lace his expression, but this time, Nik doesn't object. All I see is his back as his determined stride leads him away from me and out of the room.

Leaving me alone with my father.

I'm still on the ground, waiting for another sign of what's to come when my father tosses something across the room. It lands hard in front of me, maybe a foot away and again, I'm scared shitless. My stupid heart won't quit trying to escape my chest.

This is what war is, but I don't know how much more of it I can take.

"Your journal," my father says. "You should take it while you still can." I can hardly make out his words, let alone what the item is with the adrenaline and fear spiking through me. My sketch notebook I've long lost, the notebook that started all of this.

I'm still struck with betrayal at the knowledge that it was

Nikolai. That all this shit started with him luring me out and letting me believe it was someone I loathed, someone who would have damaged it just to get a rise out of me, or worse, burned it or thrown it away, simply because he could. Knowing it wasn't Mika, and that it was Nikolai makes me hold the sketchbook tighter. I believe in fate and that everything happens for a reason.

The front cover is nothing special. Merely an array of wildflowers painted in watercolors. It came that way. But inside its pages are sketches of the world I used to live in. The one kept safe in the confines of my bedroom on the other side of the estate. Fantasies I dared to dream. And lives I've never lived.

As I stare at the journal, I realize how much has changed so quickly. But one thing never has. It will never change.

"I thought there would be clues as to where you'd gone," my father tells me, explaining why he has it. Nikolai stole it from me. As I crawl closer to it, clutching it close, I'm still reeling from his confession.

"Is Mom's picture still inside?" I somehow get the courage to ask him.

My father only stares at me, a hard gaze that I can't place. It's almost shame, almost hate that comes from him and I don't know why. He doesn't answer me, forcing me to swallow with a dry mouth and throat as I scoot closer to the notebook and let the pages flick by my fingers until they land on the same spot I'd last seen. The one where I drew her, but the picture isn't there.

Just as the sharp gouge in my chest seems to deepen, the edges of the pages fall from the pad of my thumb until they stop, revealing the picture tucked tightly just behind the front cover.

The kind eyes of my mother gaze at me, in black and white, and the memories of her dance in the back of my mind. When the days were not as long and filled with the terror they bear today.

Back when I knew I was safe and loved and nothing bad would happen, and yet it was all a lie.

With a small, sad smile, I swallow the dryness in my throat and pick up the picture to show my father, while whispering a ragged, "Thank you."

A cold prick sweeps over my shoulders, causing a shudder to run down my spine until I tuck the photo back away. It's an odd feeling. One that reminds me of how I felt in the bathroom this morning in Carter's room. A feeling like someone else is here.

"She was always so beautiful." My father's statement is hard. Not an ounce of emotion given to the words. Again my eyes find her photo on the wall, a younger version of my mother, hung beside the photo of Carter's home.

"She was," I speak without consent and then nod my chin toward the wall, and as I do, someone yells from down the hall. It sounds more like a command than anything else, somewhere off in the distance, but it's all I've heard since the ground stopped shaking.

I wait a moment, my body still, wanting to know more of what's going on, but my father doesn't hesitate. He doesn't seem to react at all to what's going on outside of this room, and I don't understand why.

"That's not the photo you keep looking at," he says and the chill comes back to me, like the edge of an ice cube running down the back of my neck. "Did he show you a picture too? The picture of his house?"

My stomach churns as I nod once, forcing my gaze to meet my father's. "Yes," I breathe the word, drawing strength from the truth and feeling an edge of defiance I didn't know I had. "Why do you have it?" I ask him evenly, slowly standing, and gripping the notebook tightly in my right hand.

"The same reason I've hung all these photos here. They're the failures that led to my demise," he tells me, turning to look at the pictures and ignoring me. "Each one of them, my mistakes."

I can feel the agony rip through me as I look back to my mother. To the picture of her with my uncle and my father. Swallowing thickly, I try to speak but I can't.

His finger taps on the glass of the picture frame, the one of Carter's house that was destroyed. "I should have made sure they'd all died that night. When I hung this, I thought they'd be the ones to kill me. They still may be. Maybe tonight even."

A part of me wishes to console my father, to assure him that it's going to be all right. But it would only be lies, and he knows better than that.

"Are they the ones who are here?" I manage to ask him, hiding my desperation to know and why I want to know. Anxiety whispers along every inch of my skin.

My father's smirk makes his eyes wrinkle and the rough chuckle is accompanied with the telltale cough that comes from a smoker's lungs. While I was away, praying he'd come save me, I forgot how old my father's become in the past few years.

"Yes, of course they are." His answer is what I'd hoped, although I know I shouldn't. My heart hammers and my pulse quickens, but I don't show my father anything. I give him no indication of how that knowledge makes me feel.

At my lack of shock, my lack of emotion, not knowing how to react as thoughts race through my mind, my father offers me a small smile and then points to the photo of my mother, tapping his finger once again, but this time on the very edge of it. Almost like he's afraid to touch it.

"You know that I love you," my father says and it's then that his voice cracks and his expression crumples. "I was never a good father, but I chose you and I thought it counted for something."

"You are a good father," I say, pushing out the words in a

shallow breath, trying to contain the guilt and fear of what's to come. I could drown in my emotions as I take a shaky step closer to him, needing to hold him as he's held me before. "I know you were hard on me, but this life is hard and I needed it." I get it now, why he always made me stand on my own. Maybe he knew this day would come sooner than I did. The day someone would take it all away from him.

"No, no, Aria," my father says as he shakes his head. His eyes search mine, not giving away any secrets but hiding every one of them.

Another yell is heard, this time farther away and it takes my attention but only for a split second until I hear my father say, "Your mother didn't belong to me. She was supposed to marry my brother."

One beat of my heart, ragged and jagged.

"She loved him and his money... his power. He was supposed to inherit everything. He was the one meant to rule."

Another beat of my heart and my father takes down the photo, the frame making an awful cracking noise as he does, the frame splintering, from being so old perhaps. I know my uncle was supposed to be the don, the head of the family. He was older than my father, but he was killed before he could take charge.

What I didn't know, is that my mother was involved with my uncle. I've never been told such a thing.

"She fell in love with you after he died?" I assume out loud.

"She was pregnant and afraid," my father says, not looking

at me at all, or the slow realization that comes to form on my face. "She needed someone to protect her after her quick affair with him, and I loved her. I wanted her."

I can't breathe, I swear to it. An unseen hand seems to strangle me as my father slowly raises his gaze to mine.

"What?" The disbelief cloaks the whisper.

"They were only together for a short time and most people had no idea. But when he was murdered, she was pregnant, alone, and with a price on her head."

"Mom?" I don't know how her name escapes me, my breath strangling me as it refuses to leave.

"I told her no one would ever know, and she accepted." The thumb of his left hand runs along the place a wedding ring would hug his ring finger. "I always wanted you. I always loved you as my own."

My head shakes on its own and my eyes go wide. Wide with shock, wide with fear in the way my father's speaking.

"I tried to love you and show you how much you were loved. Yes, I was hard on you. I was hard on you because this life is hard, but also ... you look just like your mother."

I reach behind me for something to steady me, but there's nothing.

"She never loved me." As he speaks, the soft reminiscence is instantly replaced by hate. "Until she decided she wanted more. She wanted someone else and would do anything to get away from me. She was a rat. I'm not sure how many mistakes I truly made because of your mother. Taking her in, not killing her sooner, or having her murdered."

Everything in my body is cold, the numbing kind that makes me feel like I can't be here. Like this can't be real. He didn't. He didn't have Mom killed.

"No." The word comes unbidden as fear settles deep into my bones.

"You were never a mistake, Aria. Even when I'm gone, I want you to know that. I know I was hard and cold, but it wasn't because of you. I loved you."

I can see it in his eyes, he's telling me the truth. Every bit of it. Dark and callous.

"You couldn't have," I say, but my words are weak and desperate.

The sad smile carved into his expression is riddled with agony. "She was going to have me killed, Ria. It was either her or me."

"No." My memory is warped and twisted. My reality even more so.

"I do know she was a mistake, your mother was. One that's stayed with me and still lingers in this house."

I almost call him Dad; I almost beg him to stop. To tell me everything he just said was a lie. But I can't speak a damn word. I can't even move.

"I always had to see you, though. You were a constant reminder."

Chapter 20

Carter

"One more hall," I hear Declan tell me softly from my earpiece. "Two men on the right at the corner."

The eerie calmness that comes at times like these surrounds me. With four large steps I make it to the end of the hall, stop right at the corner and wait. Listening to every sound.

Sebastian and Jase are quiet behind me, but they're there, both armed and ready with the silencers. Only Jase is marked with a splatter of blood, but each of us has killed since we slipped in through a window, shattering it during an explosion and sneaking into the dark halls of this forbidden castle.

We're moving too slow. The thought keeps my pace fast. Every second away from her is another moment something could happen to her. A moment someone could take her away from me.

It doesn't escape my attention that I almost died here nearly a decade ago. Every quiet step reminds me of what may have been had my life been cut short.

Turning back to my brother, I nod and all at once, the three of us step out into the hall. Holding my breath and then letting it out, my grip on the gun tightens, the metal kicks back, and the bullet whips through the air, hitting the back of some fucker's skull. There's a sharp crack, a mist of blood sprayed against the pristine wall to my right. The bang of another bullet and then another are followed by the thumps of limp, heavy bodies falling to the ground.

"Four men coming, from behind you and another to your left. They know something's wrong," Declan says in the earpiece as the adrenaline spikes and Jase and I share a glance.

"Get her, we'll take care of them," Jase tells me, reaching up and squeezing my shoulder with his left hand. Sebastian nods, holding his gun with both hands and keeping his back against the wall as the sound of footsteps and a yell for someone to answer echoes up the long corridor.

"I'll have her soon," I tell them both, "and then I'll come back here." I don't know why, but it feels like a lie. Like I'm not coming back.

Jase gives me a smirk and quickly turns around, the faint sounds of him reloading his weapon carrying over to me.

Sebastian looks over his shoulder one last time to look at

me before he follows Jase back down the way we came.

Without them it feels different. It's not about revenge or murder. It's not about a war or a power play for territory. It's only about *her*. About Aria.

I won't fail her. I won't let her die.

Fueled by the memory of my nightmare, I move forward. Each step feels heavier, louder than before, even though I'm still silently moving through.

I'm vaguely aware of Declan telling me something, but I ignore him. He doesn't need to say a damn thing as I come up to the corner and hear voices.

Two voices.

Light filters under the closed door in the dark hall. And with it are the sounds of Aria pleading with her father. Begging him for something.

My heart twists into a wretched knot. That sound shouldn't exist. The pain in her cadence. It shouldn't be allowed.

My vision tricks me, giving me flashes of weeks ago. Of Aria on her knees and at my mercy. I wish I could take it back. As my hand settles on the cold steel knob of the door that mutes her cries, I wish I could take everything back.

Every piece of it. Even the moment I clung to life at the sound of her voice carrying through a closed door.

It only takes a half second for me to push the door open, the gun raised and ready to fire, but it's useless. The barrel of one already stares back at me.

"Did you really think I wouldn't be ready for you?" Talvery hisses as Aria sucks in a breath, wide eyed and backed in a corner. Tears stream down her face and I could kill the fucker now.

"Dad, please," she begs him and I can't stop looking at her, even as the sweat in my hand makes me hold the gun tighter.

"Drop your gun," he demands and the gun slips slightly in my grasp as I hear Aria whisper my name. Not in fear, not in anger. I can hear how she needs me. It won't be denied from her voice.

In my periphery, she takes a step toward me and her father cocks his gun in response. The click is resounding and foreboding. Aria stills instantly.

It's only now, in the face of actually having to make the decision, that I question if I can kill him in front of her. If I could steal her father from her.

"Don't," she begs him in a breathless whisper. She still loves me. I can feel it in the way she speaks. A piece of her still cares for me.

I tighten my grip on the gun, not knowing if she'll still love me after.

If she weren't here, he'd be dead. I could do it if she weren't here. But with her watching, still begging and hoping for the inevitable fate to change before her eyes... I'm hesitating. I've spent a decade waiting to kill this man. Waiting to make him suffer for what he did to me.

But if she hates me after... then I may as well be the one

that died.

In any other situation, I wouldn't have hesitated. Talvery would be dead simply because he took time to speak. I need Aria to love me though. A life without love is no life at all.

I don't want to die, either. I don't want her to see me die.

For the first time in years, I don't want to die. I need to protect her. I need to make it right.

"Aria." I say her name simply because I need to see her one more time. I need to know she loves me still. I need her to know it's okay. But as she looks at me, her father speaks.

"Did you think I couldn't see you?" Talvery sneers, but I don't listen to him.

"Please, Dad," Aria begs, her chest rising higher and falling deeper.

"That I didn't have backup cameras?"

All I can think, is that I need to save her. In the back of my mind, although I'm looking between Aria and Talvery, all I can see is her on the floor of my office. On her knees between my legs, cold and not breathing.

I won't let it happen.

"I'm tired and growing old. But I'm not done fighting yet. And I'm not that fucking stupid," he says lowly and I know he's going to pull the trigger. "I won't lie down and die."

"No!" Aria's scream rings through the air at the same time that he speaks his last word.

Talvery's statement again means nothing, but Aria

hurling herself forward, reaching for the gun tempting her on the corner of the desk, is everything.

Her lunge distracts both of us. But when he turns to her, I can't do anything but throw myself between the gun he points at her and the woman I need to protect. The only reason I've ever had to live.

My gun fires at him the same time his goes off, barely skimming the arm he holds the gun with as he cusses.

I don't feel the first shot. I don't even feel the second, but I see it. I see the barrel of the gun and even as the bullet flies toward me, I swear I see it. The sound of the shot is like white noise and it means nothing compared to the sound of Aria screaming. Her voice fills the room and it seems to drag across time as my heart beats slowly. Only a single beat to her long scream as she wraps her arms around me.

Her voice turns to a song, a lowly sung hum of words; I can't make out what she's saying as I stare at my chest, the bright red soaking through the crisp white shirt as I fall to the floor.

My arm doesn't brace me, it merely hits the ground hard, followed by my back and it's then that I feel the sharp twinges of pain.

I try to swallow, but blood comes up instead. A mouth full of it that spills from me as I try to say her name.

Somewhere in the back of my mind I think that I should have shot him when I first came in. I shouldn't have concerned myself with Aria. I should have killed him without thinking twice.

A dizzy sensation comes over me as my head drops back but I force my neck up, I force myself to look at Aria, to command her to get behind me, but she's not looking at me and I can't speak. Every time I try, hot blood fills my mouth. It's all I can taste; it's all I can smell. I struggle to breathe, to move even and it's not the pain. The pain is nothing. Something else is holding me down.

"No!" I hear Aria scream, but it sounds so far away.

"I'm sorry," I try to tell her, but the words are muffled as I choke on my own blood. Hate fuels me to keep my eyes open as Aria yells something I can't hear to her father. She's right here, so close to me, but I can't move my arms to hold her anymore. My body's so numb, so heavy.

I'm sorry I put her in the middle of this. I'm sorry I put her in danger. I'm sorry I made her want to run again. I'm sorry I can't protect her. That's my worst sin.

As I see the darkness settle in, the sounds fade to nothing, and her touch wanes, I'm most sorry that I can't protect her.

Fuck, no. I need to protect her still.

I don't want to leave her. I don't want to die.

"Aria," I try to say her name, but I can't.

I try to fight the heavy weight that's holding me down. "I love you," I say, but the words fail to be heard. Did I say them?

She must know them. She must.

"You can't die, Carter," I hear Aria whisper and she sounds so close but I can't see her, I can't feel her.

For the first time in so long, I'm scared. I'm terrified.

I couldn't care less about life and death. But I don't want to be without her. I need Aria. I need to protect her. And as the darkness takes over, I'm truly terrified that I'll never see her again.

The last thought I have, is that if I die, she can't die for me. Suddenly, the cold feels peaceful.

She didn't die for me. If the price to change the course of fate was that I must die for her... so be it.

Chapter 21

Aria

The blood is everywhere. My hands are stained with it as I apply pressure to the bullet wound and scream at Carter to answer me.

"Look at you." My father hasn't stopped talking, hasn't stopped shaming me for staying at Carter's side. Hasn't stopped shaming me for reaching for the gun.

I had to try. With a man on either side of me, both wanting to kill the other, I couldn't stand by helplessly, doing nothing.

The blood isn't nearly as hot as the tears that won't stop. He's not answering me; he isn't responding to me no matter how loud I scream. His name tears up my throat as I scream his name. As I do, the pressure lifts just slightly on the wound nearly in the center of his chest and more blood pools around him.

Hold him tight, or else he'll die.

Words from a man I've never met come back to me, and I shove my body down, clutching Carter and putting all of my weight on both of my hands, still compressing the wounds. "Don't leave me," I cry as my hair sticks to my wet face and the hot tears mix with his blood as I lay my cheek in the crook of his neck.

I can feel his heart.

It beats as the door to the office creaks open and my father yells at me to get up. To be a Talvery and to prove he made the right choice all those years ago. That I'm truly his daughter. His words mean nothing to me. They hang in the air. All I listen to is the faint beat of Carter's heart and how slow it is. It's slowing.

I only turn my head to look at my father when I hear him cock the gun again.

My throat is tight with emotion as I look from the barrel of the gun up to him. The pressure I have on Carter's gunshot wounds doesn't waver though.

"I love him," I plead with my father and as I do, I belatedly notice a gun laying only a foot from where I am, so close I could reach it. What a useless thing to come to me now. If I let go, Carter will die. I know it deep in my soul.

If I were to reach it, to manage to grab it and kill my father to end all of this, what point would there be in living?

I'd rather die like this, doing everything I can to save the one I love, than live knowing I let him die.

My eyes move from the gun to the portrait of his family home and I close my eyes, pressing my cheek to Carter's chest as I hold him tighter. I can't feel his chest moving anymore though. I don't hear him breathing either.

"Choose your family, Aria. Step aside and let me finish him. I forgive you," my father stresses the last sentence. Slowly, I look to him. His eyes glass over as he grips the gun tighter. "It doesn't matter what happened before, but now you need to listen to me. You need to act like the woman you were raised to be," my father tells me and instead of hearing him I only hear Tyler's words.

I can't look at my father, or the gun.

"I'm sorry," I whisper. Not to my father, but to the version of me that could have done better. To the hopes of what could have been and then I remember, I remember the small life inside of me and I cry harder. I mourn all of us and what we may have been had fate treated us better.

"Forgive me," I cry into the crook of Carter's neck and then I hear that voice again, the one I've only heard in my terrors. *Hold him tight, or else he'll die.*

"I am," I whisper to no one.

And with that I hear my father whisper how his own daughter betrayed him and then he tells me goodbye with a gunshot following close behind. The bullet is loud and it makes my shoulders jump, but I stay close to Carter, clinging to him with everything I have.

I know I heard it. I swear I did, but I felt nothing. Nothing at all.

My eyes open slowly, and I'm too afraid to breathe. I know I heard him shoot, but it didn't hit me. A long moment passes before I hear a body fall. First a thud and then a louder thump. I have to turn around, to face the desk to see my father, laying on his belly on the floor, his eyes staring ahead of him but looking at nothing as blood pools around him, spilling from the hole in his cheek.

A second passes, *tick*.

I can't do anything. The scream is silent.

Another second passes, *tock*.

And that's when I notice movement from behind the desk.

My eyes travel up the suit pants, to the fitted shirt covered in blood.

Nikolai's expression isn't cold, it isn't angry. He's heartbroken as he lowers his gun and I watch him swallow.

"Do you want to tell them it was you? Or should we tell them I did it?" he asks me and his last word is strangled. He looks between Carter and myself and I can't even answer him. I can't think about anything but how long it's been since I've felt Carter's heartbeat.

A weak pulse is the only response I get at that thought.

"Help me," I plead with him.

Chapter 22

Aria

They took him away. They took him away from me. Jase pried my fingers back and Sebastian pulled me away as I screamed. The memory loops over and over again, but it's not me. I'm merely watching it happen like the scenes of a movie.

"It hurts so much," I struggle to say out loud and I don't know who can hear me because I don't even know who's around me.

"You need to change, Aria." I hear Jase's voice, and the tremors rocking through my body only pick up.

"Is he okay?" I cry the words and he lets me fall into his embrace. When I look forward, Nikolai is watching. He saved me. He saved Carter.

"They're doing what they can," is all Jase tells me in

hushed words, as if we shouldn't be talking and the tears fall, but I don't cry any longer. Instead I take in the room. I take in everyone. How did I even get down the stairs? How did I get here, and why are Nikolai and my father's men in the same room with Jase and Sebastian? There are other men here too. Men from both sides.

My face is hot; my pulse runs fast. Before I can beg him to take me to Carter, and bring him back to see me, I hear another voice.

"This truce isn't going to last long." Brett's voice carries through the room along with the sound of several guns.

The sound of guns raised quickly behind me, and seeing guns on all sides, heats my blood.

"Put them down." The words are torn from me and I'm quick to push Jase away. I'm walking on shaky legs, but with purpose until I rip the gun from his hand.

This war is over.

The bloodshed is over.

I'm fucking done with it.

A look of shock is written on Brett's face, but I have no mercy for him. There is no mercy for anyone, not anymore.

"There's been more than enough death today."

Carter. My heart rips in half at the thought of him dying. He's barely hanging on and I'm not by his side. I can't stop seeing his face. Or hearing the way he said my name.

The gun is hot in my hands and I turn to my left. Standing

in front of the staircase, I slam the gun down on the table, shaking the precious vase my mother used to fill with flowers when I was a child. I declare, "I won't allow any more to happen." The darkly spoken words leave me even though I turn to no one.

In my periphery, I barely see the men lower their guns. Their eyes burn into me, wondering if I have any authority, and I wonder the same.

This needs to end, and I need to go to Carter. It's all I can think as the emotions well up in my throat.

"We want Romano dead," Jase speaks and his voice carries through the large space and all the way up to the tall ceilings.

"Fight with me," I tell him, hardening my words and feeling the anxiety stretch in every limb I have. Every inch of my body is hot. Every pulse seems loud and hard.

"Someone needs to pay for all this. And that man is Romano," I whisper to Jase, although it's loud enough for all in this room to hear.

"My father is dead, but I won't let anyone else die, not on your side," my voice tightens as I tell him, looking Jase in the eyes, "and not on mine. Is that understood?"

Jase's lip quirks. "It is," he says, and then turns to Nikolai.

"What about your father?" Brett asks me.

"He betrayed my mother and his loyalty," I speak up although my words are choked. I don't know what to think or believe; all I know is that he's dead and my mother is never coming back. I don't have any answers, I'll never have a way to acquire them. "My father's reign is over, and that's all that matters."

"Who reigns now?" someone to my right asks and the room resonates with the sound of shifting feet.

"We reign together." I don't hesitate to speak up. My voice is clear and carries strong conviction. "Until Romano is ten feet under, that's the top priority for all of us." I feel lightheaded with the tense air and the lack of a clear answer. "Right?" I push out the word, daring either Nikolai or Jase to disagree.

"Cross." The word is practically spit from Nik's mouth and the air thickens and practically suffocates me as I watch the men meet face to face.

"What's the status of your war, Hale?" It's been a while since I've heard anyone call Nikolai by his last name.

"My war?" he asks with a crease in his forehead, stepping up to Jase.

"I don't want to fight," Jase tells him easily, letting his tense shoulders fall and moving his hand away from his gun. My heart pitter-patters and Nik steps back slightly. "I agree with Aria," Jase says and swallows thickly, looking Nikolai in the eyes. "I side with her on this. We all fight together."

"You were on his side before," Nikolai comments as whispers spread through the room like wildfire. The hissing of the words doesn't stop when Jase speaks up along with Sebastian, explaining that Romano is now an enemy and they would rather side with me and my family than with Romano any longer.

"I have to admit, I'm surprised to still see you here," Brett says after a moment of quiet to Sebastian. "It's been a long time since you've come around." The air between the two of them is easy. They must know each other. Maybe from a time before this, I'm not sure.

"I chose my side."

"And what side is that?"

"The one with Aria."

My cousin's lips kick up into a half smirk. "I like that side," he tells Sebastian.

"You need men?" Jase asks and Nikolai answers, "We need guns."

"We have guns," Sebastian says easily as he leans against the wall.

"We can come to an agreement," I say to break up the conversation, ready for it to end. "There will be no more death between us." My voice carries a note of finality with it and no one disagrees as I walk to the end of the staircase, staring up its vacant space as I grip the railing.

The side of the house it leads to gives me an eerie feeling. A sickness in my gut. A fear that doesn't come from logic or truth.

The type of fear that lingers and creeps up on you. A fear of what has passed and is no longer. Death is stained in these halls. And with death, darkness.

"Where is Carter?" I ask and turn quickly, facing each man who was in that room, each man who pried me away from Carter as he lay on the floor, bleeding out with no sign of stopping.

Nikolai doesn't answer, and neither does Sebastian. The men on my father's side are quiet, but they watch me. I don't care if they do.

They should all know. I love him. I chose him.

"We didn't have time for the doctor to come to us. He's in the hospital," Jase answers me.

"And?" I ask, the word barely spoken.

"And we're waiting."

I won't cry in front of these men. I won't cry with an army watching my every move, an army who need strength and decisiveness. So I only nod.

"Aria, I'll handle this," Sebastian tells me and my cousin nods at him.

"What do we do with the house?" Connor asks. I've just learned he's Nik's second-in-command. "The cops may stay back, but reporters are going to come soon."

The men start to talk. A few at once, and I cut them all off.

"Burn it down." The words come from a place of hurt. A place of pain. "Burn this house to the ground," I give each word the hate they've earned before turning calmly to the men, still gripping the railing and telling them, "It was a house fire... and nothing more."

Silence and shock greet me. The house is eerily quiet, and from this day on, that's all it will ever be.

I don't know if these men will stick to the quick truce we've made or what will happen once I leave, but I'm done with all of it. The useless killing and the constant threats especially.

Before a single man can respond, I hold Jase's gaze and demand, "Take me to him." Finally releasing the railing, I step forward, my pace confident even as I fall apart, and head to the door. My stride doesn't slow and it doesn't wait for anyone.

I need Carter.

The war has changed; the players have transitioned, and pawns have been taken.

None of it matters if he dies though.

I need Carter.

Are you okay?

I stare at the message on my phone for the longest time. The hospital's waiting room is vacant with the only exceptions being Addison and myself. I only left Carter's side because the nurse said I had to. Only four people are allowed to be in the room at one time. Sebastian and Carter's three brothers wanted to see him and I'd been in there since the moment we got here. It's been ten hours now.

I slept by his side, my hand in his and my cheek on the edge of his bed. I was only in and out of sleep though and each time I fell to the depths of a dream, he was there, waiting for me.

He holds me in my dream and tells me it's okay. But it's not. It's not okay. And I tell him that over and over again. He needs to come back to me. I need him here. I can't live without him.

With tears clouding my vision, I look at the message again and instead of answering Nikolai, I ask him the same.

Are you?

It took me a while to message him back, but his reply is immediate: *My answer depends on yours.*

"You okay?" Addison asks, breaking the silence in the room. The only sound is a clock at the far end of the waiting room clicking each time the numbers change. It mocks us.

Swallowing down the ragged lump in my throat, I grab her hand when she reaches for mine and I squeeze tight, but then I let her go, moving it back to my phone. "Just a message," I answer her weakly. Everyone asks if I'm okay, as if that's even a possibility right now.

Wiping under my eyes gently with the sleeve of the baggy black hoodie Sebastian gave me, I shake my head.

"I'm right here," Addison says with a weak smile that doesn't last. It merely flickers on her face.

"And I'm here for you," I tell her back and she leans into me, resting her head on my shoulder for just a moment before bringing her knees into her chest and wrapping herself in the blanket Daniel gave her. The waiting room is so cold. But I suppose it's better that way.

I didn't expect for this to happen. I finally answer Nik.

For what? he asks.

I want to tell him – all of it. To be taken, to fall in love, to learn who I am and what I want. I haven't told Addison or anyone about the baby. Only a nurse, who I confided in because I was scared with everything that had happened. I was scared the baby would be gone. She said she wouldn't be able to tell me unless I was at least six weeks pregnant. So now, it's a matter of waiting.

It's all a matter of waiting.

Talk to me. Where are you? Nik messages me.

Hospital. He's not okay. As I write the last word and press send, that sick feeling of loss weighs me down.

You really love him? Nik answers me with the question and I don't wait to tell him that I do. To admit it.

I want to stay with him, Nikolai. I need him to be okay.

I wait and wait this time as he types but doesn't send anything. All I'm given is a bubble of dots, letting me know he's there, but the words don't come.

I don't want to lose you, I write to him before he can answer. I can feel him slipping away in my heart. As if him realizing I truly love Carter and Carter loves me, is the last string breaking that once held us together.

He'll never let us be friends. If I was him, I wouldn't.

I know he's right, but it hurts. Saying goodbye is never easy.

I won't work under him, Aria. I have to leave.

I don't even know if he'll be all right, I message him back. It's selfish of me to want for him to be there for me, even knowing this is goodbye, but Nikolai has always let me be selfish. He's always loved me. And I'll forever love him. Just not the way I love Carter, and he deserves for someone to love him that way. Everyone needs someone to love like this. With your whole body and soul. To be consumed by it.

He'll be okay. Carter knows how to fight. And there's no way he'd let me have you. He'll come back just to keep me from you.

Nik's words break me. I know this will be the end of us and whatever we had. All he'll ever be anymore is a memory.

I'll always be here for you, but you have to reach out to me. I won't be something that comes between the two of you. I'm here for you, but when he comes back to you, you know I can't be there anymore.

I love you, is all I can tell him. My last words to him.

Always, he messages back. His last words to me.

He's right. I already know Nikolai is right. Whether he's just a friend or more, doesn't matter. It's either Nikolai or Carter and between the two, there's no decision to be made. It was always Carter.

But he needs to come back to me.

"I need you," I whisper the words, gripping my phone in both of my hands as I lean forward, praying to anyone who will listen.

The last time the doctor came out, they said the surgery was done. It's only a matter of whether or not he'll wake up. And they don't know that he will.

He can't leave me like this. It's all I keep thinking. How selfish am I in this moment, but I am. I need him. Carter can't leave me. He can't leave me alone. Not when it's finally over. My hand slips to my belly. Not when I didn't even tell him he has another life to care for.

My bottom lip wobbles as I let my head fall back against the hard wall and stare up at the stark white ceiling of the waiting area outside Carter's room.

"I need you," I whimper the words and I don't know if I'm speaking to Carter, the man I love who can do nothing but try to survive, or my mother. Praying to her to do something. To save him and to keep me from being left alone in this cold world.

"I need you," the whispered plea that comes from me is ragged as I close my eyes.

The last time I spoke these words like this was when I held my mother's dead body as she lay on the floor. In the room above where my father used to work.

My eyes slowly open as Carter's story comes back to me.

He said I knocked on the door.

He said I told my father I needed him.

He claims it was my voice.

And all the while I thought he was wrong because I never went to that side of the house. Not since I last spoke those very words and my mother died. All because I swear I used to feel her there. I never roamed to that side; it scared me to even think of going, because I felt her and I know she was angry. Bitter and waiting for something I couldn't give her.

Slowly the twine unravels in my mind. The truth pricks chills down my spine.

I don't know who knocked on the door. I don't know if that's why my father stopped and let Carter go or not.

But I know where those words came from.

How could my words, spoken on the floor above Carter when my father nearly beat him to death, be echoed years later? How could he have heard my pleas and think they were meant for him?

I never knocked on the door, that wasn't me, but I did cry out, "I need you." Only it was years before Carter would ever be brought into the room beneath the bedroom where my mother was murdered.

Those words were given to my mother. I spoke them, I know I did.

But they weren't for Carter. They were never meant for him or my father.

Years later, I think my mother gave them to him. She gave them to a vulnerable boy on the brink of death, so close to the edge of a place she lingered. She gave them to him, a helpless boy caught in a horrid place, who would turn into a ruthless, merciless man. And he would one day, give her revenge in return.

The story is there, tickling the edge of my mind, and it keeps me frozen in my seat, gripping the edge of the chair.

The last few months play out in my head, slow motion for some moments, and only glimpses for other scenes.

The only reason I fell into Romano's trap was because Nikolai took my drawing pad… the one that had my mother's picture in it.

I only fought for it because of the picture.

Swallowing is futile; my pulse quickens and an anxiety I haven't felt since I ventured into the east wing of my father's house returns. The wing where my mother died.

I remember the way I felt when I stabbed Stephan. My skin felt like ice. And there was a hand, a hand over mine that wouldn't stop. I couldn't stop stabbing him. The thought is sobering to my tired mind. The exhaustion that weighs my eyelids down seems to vanish as I try to swallow, each of the events that have led me to this point falling into place in my mind like puzzle pieces.

A chill spreads over my skin as I hold on to the armrest of the chair with a white-knuckled grip. My blood runs even colder, and I can't shake it. I can't shake the freezing fear that flows through me. It's something unnatural and my thoughts make no sense. It's not truth. It's not real. It's only a coincidence.

Still, I turn slowly, ever so slowly to Addison and ask her, barely breathing the words, "Do you think the ones we lost stay with us forever in some way?"

"Ria," Addison breathes out as she takes my hand in both of hers, freeing it from gripping the armrest and pats the top of it soothingly. "He's going to make it," she says and her voice is hoarse with emotion.

I shake my head, rubbing under my eyes with the hand she doesn't have and telling her, "No, not him. Not Carter." A second passes, one painful beat in my chest before I look into her soft gaze and ask, "Do you think others, others we loved but who have passed stay with us?"

She searches my gaze for only a moment before nodding her head.

"They must." Her answer is final with no room for doubt.

At the same time as the doctor walks through the doorway, heading straight to us, Addison adds, "Even death can't sever love."

Chapter 23

Carter

She was here. I know it. I can still smell the soft citrus scent of her shampoo. As death threatened to drag me to hell where I belong, I swear I heard her sing for me. The cadence of her sweet, feminine voice, carried past the damnation I knew was sure to come and I clung to it.

I will forever cling to her.

I could hear her, even feel her, but I couldn't open my eyes. I couldn't speak either. All I wanted to do was to tell her I love her. But I couldn't.

I would rather her pull a gun out on me any day than to lose her.

Knock, knock. The door creaks open as the knocks filter into the room.

A trot in my chest proves I'm still waiting on Aria, but it's not her. My brothers come in, but Aria's not here. For a split second, I think maybe it was all in my mind. That she wasn't here at all.

Maybe it was only a dream.

Fear consumes every piece of me. She didn't die in my place. Aria can't die. No!

"Aria," I breathe her name and Sebastian tells me she's okay. She's in the hall waiting.

A sharp pain shoots through my chest, a pain I've never felt before and I can hear the beeping of a machine over and over as I grimace.

"You don't have to sit up," Daniel tells me, moving to my side and trying to keep me from moving. I want to go to her. To see her. "Don't overdo it," I hear Jase tell me. As my head starts to feel lighter, I focus only on breathing.

"Fuck off," I say and shove him away, ignoring the heat of an agonizing pain rip up my right side. I seethe inwardly and in that moment, at this weak moment in my life, the door opens and Aria's there.

It's all like a dream. My body slumps back, my focus entirely on her and the way her eyes lift to mine, brightening at the sight of me looking at her.

"Just relax," Jase tells me as he drags a chair across the room, cutting off my path to Aria for a split second and again I try to get up and go to her, but it fucking hurts.

Daniel tries to push me back down, a gentle push, but he can fuck off.

He doesn't need to do a damn thing anyway; the pain is enough to keep me from moving. It's such a sharp pain, I can feel it everywhere. It heightens the slight twinge from the needles in my arm. The pressure on my chest feels like too much.

All of this pain is negligible though. She's here. We survived.

"I'm fine," I grit through my teeth, refusing to take my eyes away from her.

"Have it your way," Daniel says then raises his hands and backs up to lean against the wall in front of me. His head rests against the cream walls, next to a painting of some church. Seeing it reminds me where I am. The doctor came in a moment ago. Saint Francis Hospital is small and off a back road. They're also now equipped with two dozen men outside this room, this hall, and this building.

The doctor said I need at least a week in bed. I'll give it two days.

I want to be home. With Aria.

I won't stay here for long.

"How are you doing?" Jase asks me and I give him a side-eye.

"Fucking peachy," I answer him. My heart tightens as I watch Aria take a half step closer. Her fingers wring around one another nervously. She's still quiet and hasn't said a word.

I remember those last moments, but I also remember that she ran away.

And the last time we were alone... I remember that too. How she cuffed herself to the bed at my command. At my arrogance.

Never again. I'll never let it happen again.

"What happened?" I hate that I have to ask and the knot in my throat nearly suffocates me knowing that regardless of what happened when I blacked out, my songbird went through it alone. I wasn't strong enough for her.

I failed her.

My throat constricts when Jase tells me Nikolai killed her father. He shot him and now we have a truce. One built on the condition that we join forces to eliminate Romano.

Nikolai was her knight in shining armor. I knew I'd owe him, but I never imagined I'd owe him for my own life.

"Romano is the new target then," I tell Jase with a tight voice, letting go of the jealousy and the hate I have for the first love Aria ever had. I force the semblance of a smirk to my lips as I shift on the bed. Every movement exacerbates the pain of the needles digging into my arms.

I needed a blood transfusion. Three ice cold bags of the shit. I may not have been able to speak or even open my eyes. But I felt it. I felt everything as I hovered the edge of death, fighting to get back to Aria, moving toward the sound of her mournful hums.

"It's the right move to go after Romano. We can let Talvery's men choose what position they take afterward, but for now, Romano is the only enemy," Jase says and Daniel agrees.

"I know." I swallow gravely and watch Aria in my periphery. My brothers may be in front of me, but I couldn't give two shits about them. I don't care about the war. The territories. I don't care about anything other than never putting Aria in the line of fire again.

"He knows we fucked him." Jase's voice is even as he slips his hands into his pockets. I can see through his jeans how he balls them into fists before releasing them and then does it all over again as he speaks.

My heartbeat is faint and the voices around me are nothing but muted white noise as I stare at him. The soft beeps of the monitor continue all the while I have to force myself to focus on what they're saying.

All I want to do is make sure we're all right. I need to know that Aria and I are all right and that she forgives me. For everything.

I'm so fucking weak for her.

She has me in every way she can. Forever more.

"With Aria being seen and involved, the Talvery men won't turn on us." He peeks over his shoulder and pauses, seemingly biting his tongue before adding, "For now."

I gauge Aria's response, but she gives away nothing. Nothing at all. Her small frame doesn't even sway as she keeps her focus on me. On the tubes that connect to the needle in my veins and the monitors on my chest. I wish I could rip the fuckers out right now. I don't want her to see me like this.

I may be weak for Aria, but I won't be like this, confined to this bed, for long.

"Nikolai won't betray us so long as he thinks Aria is safe," Jase says.

"Nikolai won't betray us," Aria speaks for the first time, her voice hard as she gives her full attention to Jase, daring him to deny what she's saying is true. "He'll keep his word."

"The war between our families is over. We'll act as one." Aria's strength and determination are barely offset by the raw emotion in her voice. The reluctance to accept anything else will be her downfall. But I'll catch her. And I will bend to her volition as best I can.

"For now," Daniel speaks up. "Someone from your ranks may want to go their own way, to take men and rally against you, Aria. But for now, Nikolai is on our side. And even if they split off, we can let them. We don't need to fight for their territory."

Aria assesses him, her chest not moving as she refuses to breathe. With a single nod, she gives way to what may happen. I've seen it before, small factions separating. Generally, it ends with bloodshed, but we'll handle that when the time comes.

Jase holds her stare for only a moment before nodding once. "Either way," he speaks to me, "Romano is a dead man. He can hide in his safe house all he wants. I'll find him. I'll kill him."

"Another day and the enemies change," Daniel comments.

"We can talk about it once you're feeling better," Jase says.

"You and Sebastian handle this, plan the attack, but keep me informed." The ease with which I give up control shocks Jase, if his raised eyebrow is any indication.

"I have other things to attend to." As I speak, my hand grips the edge of the bed and I wish it was Aria's hand. I need her close to me. I need to know every piece of us fits back together how it should, how it was meant to all along.

I need her to love me.

That's all I need.

"One more thing," Jase tells me, rocking on his heels just as Daniel kicks off the wall, ready to leave us alone. Jase can't get the fucking hint.

"What?" I don't hide my annoyance in the curt response. But it only makes both of my brothers smile.

"Do you remember that woman in the Red Room?" Jase asks me and I feel the pinch in my forehead as I shake my head no.

He lets out an exasperated sigh but says it doesn't matter. "Her sister is the girl we met in the Red Room. Jennifer something. She died and her sister is causing a scene. She's making threats and calling the cops."

"Who is she?" I ask him, wondering why the fuck we

should care. Plenty of assholes call the cops on us when they don't know any better. We pay the cops to tell us exactly who and why. And we pay them well.

"The sister of the girl who wound up dead. The one we questioned about the SL stash bought in bulk."

I peek at Aria, who squirms where she stands, her gaze shifting from me to Jase.

"And?" My heart races, wondering what she's thinking.

"I figured I'd stop by and see what she knows."

"And how are you going to get that information?" Aria asks, again speaking up but only to make her presence known as well as her newfound authority.

"Don't worry, Miss Talvery," Jase rolls her name off her tongue, "I'll be a gentleman."

"I don't believe you," she tells him but the hint of a smile graces her lips.

"Do you need someone to come with you?" Daniel asks and it's only then that I realize how tired he is. How tired they all are.

"I can go on my own – I just wanted you to know," he tells Daniel and then looks back at me.

It's quiet in the room for a moment and every second that passes, I wonder if he's all right. Ever since Marcus told us the truth about Tyler's death, sadness and despair have clouded Jase's eyes.

"Are you okay?"

Agony ripples through his dark blue eyes, but he plays it off. He's always handled hardship that way. "You're asking me when you're the one strapped to a fucking bed?"

"I'll only be here for a day or two." I keep my voice low and warning. "Remember that."

Daniel's chuckle is genuine, but Jase's smile doesn't reach his eyes.

"Yeah, I'm fine. Why?"

Shaking my head, I say, "Nothing."

"Is that all?" Daniel asks Jase and he responds by holding up a finger. He goes on to tell me about the money coming in and how the last week's been fucked. How another shipment of sweets was stolen. I don't fucking care anymore. I just don't care. He can take on the problems now.

All the while Jase speaks, Aria's eyes don't leave me. I can feel her gaze burning into me. My flesh. My very soul.

"Could you guys give us a minute?" I ask my brother as a spike of pain ricochets up my right side, from my toes to my hip and up the back of my shoulder and down the front. My entire body is in agony.

But it's my chest that hurts the most. The pain that fills the vacant hollowness of my chest where there should be warmth. I finally look at Aria, letting my gaze roam down her small body. Her thin cotton shirt is wrinkled, presumably from waiting in the chairs all this time for me to wake up.

Please God, let her have waited for me. It must mean

something for her to be here. I don't remember everything that happened, but I'm sure I told her I loved her. I'm certain if ever there were words I would utter as death came to take me away, they would be only those that spoke of what she meant to me. *Everything.*

"I need to speak with Aria."

Chapter 24

Aria

"Please forgive me." I've asked him so many times tonight. This time it's to his face while he's conscious, not while his eyes are closed and he's far away from me, close to death's door and never able to hold me again.

The second the door closed, I couldn't help but to plead once more for him to forgive me. "I shouldn't have left." I let the words fall from my lips as I make my way closer to him.

He has the darkest eyes I've ever seen, but the specks of silver pierce into me... always. The way he looks at me, as if I only exist to be consumed by him, will haunt me until the day I die. And I wouldn't have it any other way.

I'm dying inside being this far away from him. I need to touch him, to hold him and make sure he's really here. My heart doesn't believe he's all right. And it hurts inside of me like no other pain I've ever felt.

"As long as you forgive me, I'll forgive you of any and every sin you've ever dared commit. Just love me. All I want is you, Aria. I can't lose you." His last words are strained, the pain of his wounds showing even with the steady drip of the IV forcing painkillers into his veins.

I can't even think about forgiving him, knowing it didn't have to end like this. I didn't have to run. It seems childish now, standing in front of him, seeing the consequences of my fear and my rash decision to hide the truth from him and flee from it all.

"Carter," I say, and his name is a tortured word on my tongue. "I'm so sorry," I utter painfully as I reach for him, getting closer to the hospital bed and letting my hand fall onto his forearm. My legs are weak; I'm barely able to stand seeing him like this.

My beast, hooked up to a machine and riddled with pain. All because of me and my foolishness.

"Forgive me," I can barely get the words out, letting everything between us fall. Every pretense, every wall. There's no room for any of it between us. "I shouldn't have run from you."

"I forgive you." His deep voice is raw. "I already told you I have. All I want is you."

All the words I wanted to tell him are strangled in the

back of my throat, refusing to come out at the sight of him.

"We aren't perfect. And if I could, I'd go back and change the way we came to be, but I'll be damned if I'd let you go."

He's saying everything I dreamed he'd say, but I still have to tell him and I can't.

I can't bear to tell him why I left.

"It's okay, songbird," Carter tells me, soothing me and luring me to come even closer. "I love you," he whispers and that breaks me. Finally, and completely, I break for him. Every piece of me shatters.

And I've never felt more complete in my life. Thoroughly ruined for the man I love.

There's one secret left. One small truth that could change everything. And it won't be kept hidden any longer.

"Do you want to know something?" I ask him, feeling the tension in my body increased with anxiety. The secret I've been holding is going to swallow me whole unless I give it the freedom to be spoken.

With his gaze tired, the exhaustion of everything weighing down the strength Carter possesses, he brushes my cheek with his knuckles, and I take his hand in both of mine.

"Anything and everything," he tells me and lets out a deep exhalation.

With a small smile wavering on my lips, I let out the secret just beneath my breath, "I think I'm pregnant. That's why I ran." The secret punctures my chest, creating a crater so deep it will never be filled if Carter's reaction doesn't mend the wound. "I didn't know what to do."

He may forgive me for keeping it from him. But I never will. In this moment, seeing and feeling with every piece of me how much he loves me, I can't believe for a moment I ever dared to not tell him. To hide this from him.

A second passes and a thump in my chest feels raw and painful as pain and betrayal flash in his eyes.

"Pregnant?" he questions and I can only nod.

In the seconds that tick by without a response from him, without knowing what he's thinking, the pain trickles into my veins and I creep closer to Carter, needing him to give me something.

"I'm sorry," I whisper the words, feeling the remorse consume me. I was going to run away, and take his child with me. Tears fall freely down my cheeks. If he hated me, I would understand; there's no way I would ever forgive him had he dared to do the same to me.

There's a moment when someone looks directly into your soul, and you feel what they feel. The loss, the insignificance, the agony of being alone. I can feel it from him as he looks up at me and I can't stand seeing it. My hand finds his and I squeeze it with both of mine, needing him to know I'm here now. "I don't want to leave, and I regret it. I regret ever walking out that door," I plead with him. And he squeezes my hand back before bringing my wrist to his lips and leaving a slow, tender kiss there. A kiss that feels like goodbye.

Finally, he speaks and it's nothing that I ever expected. "I promise I'll be a good father. I swear to you I will."

I can't speak.

"Give me a chance. Just one chance," he begs me, as if I'd ever leave his side again. "I'll be good to you, I'll be a good father, I promise." He swallows thickly.

"I'm ashamed at what I did and who I was. Please, Aria, we don't have to tell him."

"What?" I question him as I struggle to keep up with whatever he's thinking. I know he's not well now, he's still in pain and on meds. He's only just woken up. "Tell who?" I ask him, my heart racing.

"Our baby," he says as he looks up at me and brings his hand to my cheek, his thumb running under my eye to brush away the tears gathered there. "We don't have to tell them what a monster I was," he whispers the strained words and I lose all composure, covering my mouth with my hand and falling into him. I'm mindful of my weight and make sure to keep it off of him, but my God do I need him to hold me. And I need to hold him.

In this moment and forever.

"I love you, Carter," is all I can manage when I finally look up to him.

My breath and words leave me as a heat flows over me, taking every bit of the bitter cold and banishing it from me. I crash my lips to Carter's and he's quick to cradle my head with his hand, pinning me to him and deepening the kiss. His tongue slips between my lips and I grant him entry. Our tongues mingle and he massages mine with swift, possessive strokes.

I don't breathe until he breaks away.

"I would do anything for you." He says the words as if they're a confession. "I swear, you are the only thing that matters to me. Nothing else matters. Only you and our baby." As he speaks, his hand slips to my waist. He gazes at my midsection as if he can already see me swollen with our child. The very vision is what caused me to run in the first place.

"I'm scared." The wretched confession makes me feel that much weaker.

"Don't be." Carter's words are simple, but impossible.

"I don't know what's going to happen," I tell him, feeling the raw truth of fear lingering in the statement.

Carter's eyes search mine as I climb into the small bed with him, needing to be closer to him and not giving a shit if there's barely any room. I need my body pressed to his. I need to feel him breathing. The second he embraces me, my worries slip away, lost in the haze of knowing I'm where I'm supposed to be. Beside Carter Cross. Our present and our future tied together.

"We will rule. That's what's going to happen, my songbird."

I can feel my heart twist in my chest, praying I'll be the

woman he wants me to be. Praying our lives can't pull us apart anymore. And as my mind whirls with every possible outcome of what could be, I realize there's not a damn thing that could tear me away from him. Not one fucking thing.

"Marry me. You belong with me, Aria." Carter's dark eyes pin me in place, taking my breath and refusing to give it back. "Marry me," he repeats lowly, a barely spoken yet desperate whisper. His warm breath cradles my cheek as he lowers his lips to mine and gently kisses me before I can answer. With his forehead leaning against mine and his hand gripping my hip in place, he whispers his plea again. "Marry me."

I cling to him, burying my head in his chest and breathing in the scent of a man I'm madly in love with as I nod my head and let the ragged whisper leave me with the desperation for all of this to be real, "Yes." He's alive. He's with me. And he wants me as his partner, his wife, his love.

He lifts my head with both of his hands on my face and presses a soft kiss to my lips. It's only then that I taste the salt of tears I hadn't known I was shedding.

"You're everything to me," he whispers against my lips as he brushes away the tears with his thumb.

"Tell me everything is going to be all right," I beg him. My words beg him. My body caves to his in the way it's always willed me to. The moment I saw him, I knew deep in the marrow of my bones that I belonged to this man. The other half to my soul. Holding his life to mine is the worst thing

I've ever felt in this world. Every second that passed, I was afraid to move, knowing he was bleeding out beneath me. He lost so much blood, he barely made it and I can't help but to think that if I'd made the wrong move, if I hadn't held him as tightly as I could for as long as I did, he wouldn't be here anymore. I would have lost him.

"I never want you to leave me again. Never," I whisper the last word, pushing myself closer to him; every inch of me that can be pressed against him is. And Carter does what he's best at. He keeps me close, holding me to him as if I'll fly away if only he loosened his grip. But I'll never do that again. Never.

"As long as you love me, it will." His words are whispered along my skin, sending a trail of goosebumps down my body as he plants a small kiss on my shoulder. "Because I love you." His rough stubble grazes my shoulder, and I hope it scars me. I hope I can feel him, see him, have evidence of his love forever.

"I love you, Carter." The truth is the easiest thing to speak in this moment. A raw confession that will save us from whatever is to come.

"I love you, songbird." His rough voice is deep, the depths of sincerity so true, it numbs every pain inside of me. Every pain that's ever existed.

Days have passed since we came home.

It's odd to think of this place as home, but that's all it is to me now. It's more of a home to me than my father's place ever was. Simply because of the people in it.

"You need to take it easy." I try to keep my voice from sounding like I'm nagging Carter, but every time he leans to his side on the bed to grab something from the bedside table, I see him grimace. "You're still healing."

I'm quick to reach over, careful not to put my weight on him and grab his phone for him. The vibrating of notifications is a constant, but even still, the moment I hand it to him, he silences it.

Jase and Sebastian have taken the lead while Carter's been on bedrest at home. It'll take time for the wounds to heal, even if my beast still thinks he's untouchable.

I still can't breathe around him. The fear of losing him won't leave me.

"You keep saying that," he remarks with the same evenness I give him, but the smile on his lips, the genuine happiness in his eyes, haven't left him since I told him about the baby. Every time I look into his eyes, I see it and it's so raw, so much so, that I can barely stand to hold his gaze.

"I'm serious, Carter," I reprimand him although my actions are anything but. Moving to straddle him on the bed, the sheet slips around me, puddling behind us as I settle gently in his lap and take his stubbled jaw in my hands. "I need you," I whisper.

The corners of his lips kick up, and his large hands wrap around my waist, gentle and comforting. I rest my forehead on his with my lips so close to his as he tells me, "I need you too."

He gives me a quick kiss. And then another.

"Did you take another test?" he asks me and I can hear the playfulness in his voice. He thinks I'm odd for taking a pregnancy test every day, but I have my reasons. The line is supposed to stay strong and dark, because then it means the baby is still there and until the six-week mark is here, I need the tests for my sanity.

"Yes," I tell him. I almost mention how Addison's the one who told me. She said the line gets weaker if you lose the baby. She's waiting like I am.

Instead, I'm distracted by a kiss on my neck. A languid one that makes my nipples pebble. His rough stubble runs along my skin, instantly making me wanton.

"You need to heal." I practically hiss the words with longing as his lips move to the dip just below my collar and his right hand reaches up to my breast. Plucking my nipple between his fingers, he finally raises his gaze to my eyes and tells me, "All I need is you."

He's wrong though. There's so much more he needs. Much more than I could ever give him.

He's a wounded man, with scars so deep he can't help but to be weighed down by them.

I'm still waiting on edge for something to come between us, but Carter seems hellbent on keeping us together. And so am I. I won't allow for love not to be enough.

Carter's fingertips glide easily up my neck, leaving goosebumps in their wake until he wraps his hands around my throat. His thumb runs down the underside of my chin and then lower, down to the center of my throat. His lips are parted just slightly, his breathing ragged as he hardens under me, his thick length pressing against me.

"I will do anything for you." He utters the words with such an intensity before slowly raising his gaze to meet mine.

My damn heart belongs to him. It only starts beating when he looks at me like that. I swear it's true. Whatever else it does when he's not around isn't what it's doing now.

"You're so intense," I whisper, not knowing what else to say, but my words are lost in the haze of lust that lingers between us.

I don't know if it's the fact that I'm obviously hot for him or some other reason, but Carter gives me a lazy smirk before moving the back of his fingers up my silk shirt and gently pinching my nipple.

My natural instinct is to playfully smack him away, but he's too quick, grabbing my wrist and pinning it behind me.

Even while I straddle him, he commands me.

"You make me this way," he tells me with a deep voice and leans forward to kiss me at the same time as he pinches my hardened peak. I have to gasp as he does, breaking the kiss and arching my neck. He takes the moment to lightly run his teeth along my sensitized skin, and I know I'm done for. Any authority I had over him is gone.

Carter is an untamable beast. But I'll be damned if I'd have him any other way.

"It all feels better when I'm with you," he murmurs against my skin and his tone sounds raw and hints at the pain that will forever scar who we are. With both hands on his jaw, I stare deep into his eyes, bright with sincerity. "All of it," he tells me.

"It's going to be okay." I offer him words I pray are true. I'd do anything for this man and without anything between us, nothing will keep us apart.

"Better than okay," he says before kissing me sweetly, only breaking away to add, "I promise."

Chapter 25

Jase

It was supposed to be me.

The car moves over a speed bump a little too fast, and my hard body sways in the sedan. My grip tightens on the wheel, and I try to swallow the hard lump that's been suffocating me since I learned the truth about Tyler's death.

It was a hit... on me. A fucking hoodie is the reason he's ten feet in the ground and I'm still here, taking every day for granted.

Slowing at the stop sign, I let a deep breath calm the anxiety running through me. With a war raging and an unknown enemy taking pieces of us as he pleases, I don't have time to get lost in the unfortunate past. No matter how much I long to go back. If only we could go back.

The hum of the engine as I roll over another speed bump keeps me in the present.

I shouldn't have come out right now. Spending the afternoon in the burbs isn't exactly on my normal to-do list.

But I had to get out of the house and away from my brothers. The regret and guilt and mourning that lingers in their eyes haunts me day and night.

There's nothing I can do to change it. But I can pay Beth a visit and quiet her.

My keys jingle as the ignition turns off and the soft rumble of the engine is silenced.

Wiping a hand over my face, I get out of the car, not caring that the door slams as my shoes hit the pavement. The neighborhood is quiet and each row of streets is littered with picture-perfect homes, nothing like the home I grew up in. Little townhouses of raised ranches, complete with paved driveways and perfectly trimmed bushes. A few houses have fences, white picket of course, but not 34 Holley, the home of Bethany Fawn, also known as the woman who keeps raising hell at the Red Room. More recently she's been calling the cops and demanding answers. She's the woman who blames Carter for her sister's untimely death. Her sister Jennifer, a girl we met in the Red Room weeks ago. A girl in a mess she couldn't get out of, with a drug addiction she couldn't kick.

I know all about wanting someone to blame and looking for answers to questions that don't make any difference once you have them. Bethany's hurt and angry, but she won't find any answers from us. A simple warning should scare her off.

The skin over my knuckles tightens and the cuts from a few nights before crack open, sending a pain shooting up my arm. I welcome the seething reminder that I'm alive.

Knock, knock, knock. She's in there, I can hear her. Time passes without anything but the sound of scuttling behind the door, but just as I'm about to knock again, the door opens a few inches. Only enough to reveal a peek of her.

Her chestnut hair falls in wavy locks around her face. She brushes the fallen strands out of her face to peek up at me.

"Yes?" she questions and my lips threaten to twitch into a smirk.

"Bethany?" Her weight shifts behind the door as her gaze travels down the length of my body and then back up to meet mine before she answers me.

The amber in her hazel eyes swirls with distrust as she tells me, "My friends call me Beth."

"We haven't met before... but I'll happily call you Beth." The flirtatious words slip from me easily, and slowly her guard falls although what's left behind is a mix of worry and agony. She doesn't answer or respond in any way other than to tighten her grip on the door.

"Mind if I have a minute?"

She purses her her full lips slightly as the cracked door opens an inch more to cautiously reply, "Depends on what you're here for."

My heartbeat gallops, trotting faster in my chest as the anxiety rises. I'm here to give her a warning. To stay the hell away from the Red Room and to get over whatever ill wishes she has for my brothers and me.

It's a shame really; she's fucking gorgeous. There's an innocence, yet a fight in her that's just as evident and even more alluring. Had I met her on other terms, I would do just about anything to get her under me and screaming my name.

The swirling colors in her eyes darken as her gaze dances over mine. As if she can read my thoughts and knows the wicked things I'd do to her that no one else ever could. But that's not why I'm here, and my sick perversions will have to wait for someone else.

I lean my shoulder against her hard walnut front door and slip my shoe between the gap in the doorway, making sure she can't slam it shut. Instead of the slight fear I thought may flash in her eyes as my expression hardens, her eyes narrow with hate and I see the beautiful hue of pink in her pale skin brighten to red, but it's not with a blush, it's with anger.

"You need to stay out of the Cross business, Beth." I lean in closer, my voice low and even. My hard gaze meets her narrowed one, but she doesn't flinch. Instead she clenches her teeth so hard I think they'll crack.

With the palm of my hand carefully placed on the doorjamb and the other splayed against her door, I lean in to tell her that there are no answers for her in the Red Room. I want to tell her my brother isn't the man she's after, but before I can say a word she hisses at me, "I know all about Marcus and the drug and why you assholes had her killed."

My pulse hammers in my ears but even over it, I hear the strained pain etched in her voice. Her breathing shudders as she adds, "You will all pay for what you did to my sister." Her voice cracks as her eyes gloss over and tears gather in the corners of her eyes.

"You don't know what you're talking about," I tell her as the anger rises inside of me. Marcus. Just the name makes every muscle inside of my body tighten and coil.

The drug.

Marcus.

Before I can even tie what she's said together, I hear the click of a gun and she lets the door swing open, throwing me off-balance.

Shock makes my stomach churn as the barrel of a gun flashes in front of my eyes. She leans back, moving to hold the heavy metal piece with both hands. Lunging forward, still off-balance as fear stirs in my blood, I grip the barrel and raise it above her head, shoving her small body back until it hits the wall in her foyer.

Bang!

The gun goes off and the flash of heat makes the skin of my hand holding the barrel burn and singe with a raw pain.

Her lower back crashes into a narrow table, a row of books toppling over and mail falls onto the floor as I stumble into her and finally pin her to the wall.

Her small shriek of fear is muted when I bring my right hand to her delicate throat. My left still grips the gun. She struggles beneath me but with a foot on her height and muscle she couldn't match no matter how hard she tried, it's pointless. Her heart pounds so hard, I feel it matching mine.

She yelps as I lift the gun higher, ripping it from her grasp. Both of her hands fly to the one I have tightening on her throat.

She tried to kill me. I can't fucking believe it.

Barely catching my breath, I don't let anything show except for the absolute control I have over her. The door is wide open and I'm certain someone would have heard. A faint breeze carries in from behind me and I take a step back, pulling her with me just enough so I can kick the door shut and then press her back to it. Her pulse slows beneath my grip and her eyes beg me for mercy as her sharp nails dig into my fingers. A second passes before I loosen my grip just enough so she can breathe freely.

Through her frantic intake, I lean forward, crushing my body against hers until she's still. Until her eyes are wide and staring straight into mine. The sight of her, the fear, the desperation, the eagerness to live ... it thrills a dark side of me that's been begging to be brought to the surface.

"You're going to tell me everything you know about Marcus." I lower my lips to the shell of her ear, letting my rough stubble rub along her cheek. "And everything you know about the drug."

With a steadying breath, my lungs fill with the sweet smell of her soft hair that brushes against my nose.

I comb my fingers through her hair and let my thumb run along her slender neck before I lean into her, letting her feel how hard I am just to be alive. Just to have her at my mercy.

"But first, you're coming with me."

About the Author

Thank you so much for reading my romances. I'm just a stay at home Mom and an avid reader turned Author and I couldn't be happier.

I hope you love my books as much as I do!

More by Willow Winters
www.willowwinterswrites.com/books

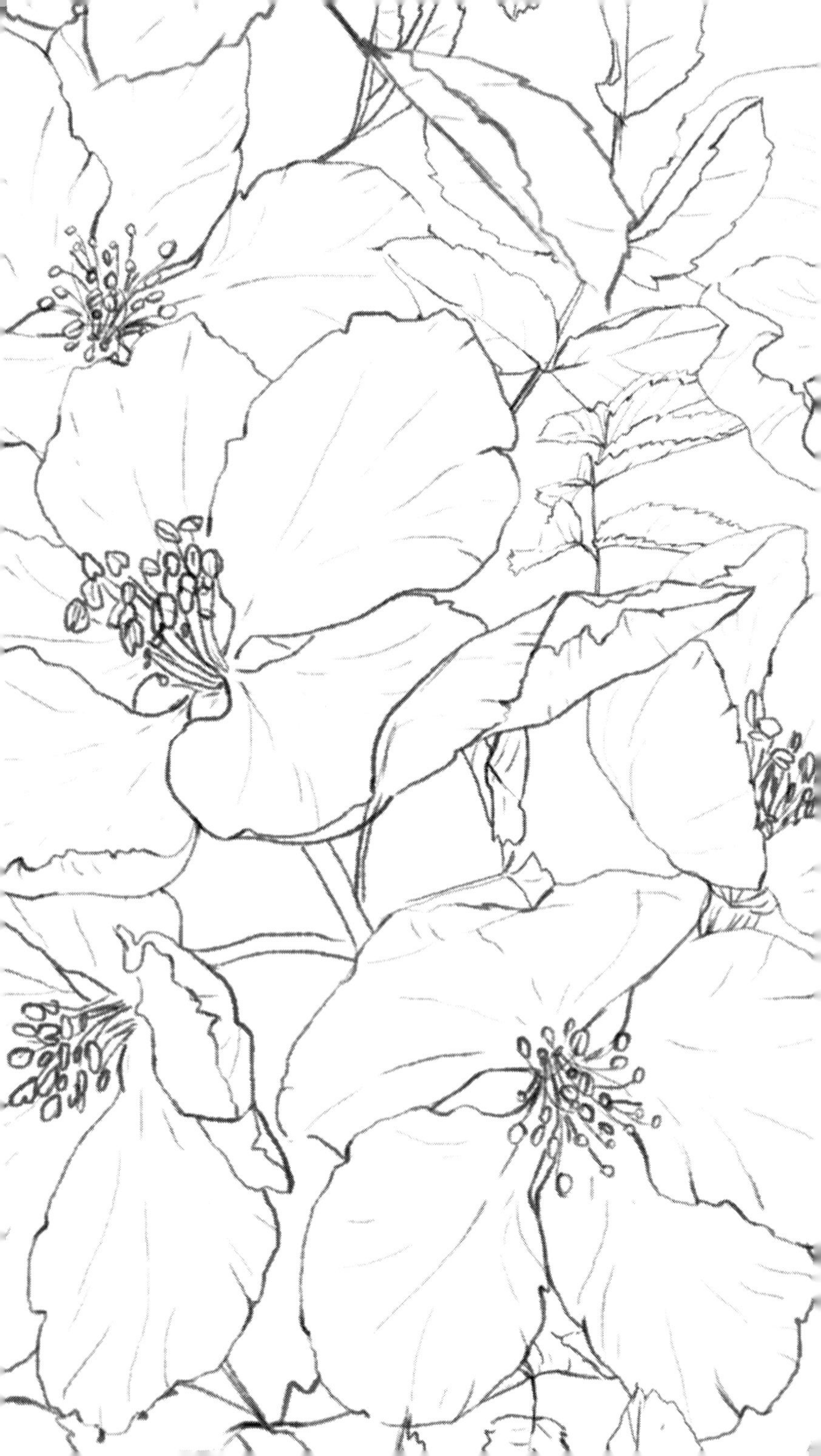

Printed in Great Britain
by Amazon